*Also by Giff Cheshire
in Large Print:*

Renegade River

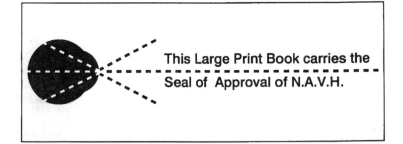

STRONGHOLD

GIFF CHESHIRE

G.K. Hall & Co. • Thorndike, Maine

Published in 1998 by arrangement with Golden West Literary Agency.

G.K. Hall Large Print Paperback Series.

The text of this Large Print edition is unabridged.
Other aspects of the book may vary from the original edition.

Set in 16 pt. Plantin by Minnie B. Raven.

Printed in the United States on permanent paper.

Library of Congress Cataloging in Publication Data

Cheshire, Gifford Paul, 1905–
    Stronghold / by Giff Cheshire.
        p.   cm.
    ISBN 0-7838-0293-5 (lg. print : sc : alk. paper)
    1. Large type books.   I. Title.
[PS3553.H38S7   1998]
813′.54—dc21   98-7916

To Mildred
wife, mother, and Girl Friday
in gratitude

CHAPTER I

It was cold on the rim, with a January wind sweeping off the Modoc basin, but Monk was enjoying himself too much to notice it. His horse was out of sight down the slope, while Monk lay on his belly at the brink of the bluff above Forbidden Canyon. His eyes, small and heated, were riveted to the figure of a girl, a young, slim figure but womanly. She was flitching a skin in the yard of a cabin, down there at the foot of the Coyote Hills.

Squaw work, he thought, and fitting, for her father had been a squaw man most of her life. But she sure was a looker. Studying the lines of her body in that position, down on her knees and bent over the hide she was scraping, he wanted to whicker. He'd horsed around with saloon girls in Winnemucca and Humboldt City who'd give their fancy garters to have looks like Wendy Dunes'. She was going to waste out here in the Wagonwheel. That was the fault of Martin Dunes more than of Wendy, however. The squaw man had been the first to come into the basin, and not only kept the latecomers away from her and their shacky place here in the canyon but also thought he owned the basin itself and regarded everybody else as squatters.

Monk let his lips pull against large teeth. The

Sleeper family never worried much about ownership. He'd got the gelding he was riding by the simple means of eliminating the Modoc Indian who'd owned it. And, by God, he was going to have that handsome filly down there, her liking it or not. Monk indulged in a chuckle that all at once died in his throat.

The chilly voice behind him said, "All right, Sleeper. On your feet and damned quick."

The lust that had heated Monk's overgrown body drained out while he pushed himself to a sitting position. He twisted his neck to see Dunes standing there, a buckskin-clothed, bearded man who held a rifle at his hip. The eyes that regarded Monk were danger-brimming pits.

"Up, damn you," Dunes said, and the rifle muzzle came a little nearer.

Monk scrambled to his feet, trying to pull onto his face the cool, derisive grin he'd admired in the tough hombre he'd seen tree a saloon in one of the railroad towns. He had a gun on his hip and could fancy himself reaching for it but had not the slightest ambition to do so. Dunes was nine parts mystery in the Wagonwheel, but everybody knew he could shoot the chirp out of a magpie's beak.

"Hell, Dunes," Monk said, his voice anything but the man-to-man tone he had hoped to muster, "I only stopped to blow my cayuse. Been up to the army camp and come back through the Coyotes. It's rough going."

8

Dunes didn't say anything.

"Know you don't like company," Monk said placatingly. "But I got curious about where you folks live and all and took me a look. No harm intended."

Even that didn't crack the rocky sternness of Dunes' face — which was a handsome face, accounting maybe for Wendy's good looks. "So you seen," Dunes said. "Now get. And if I catch you spyin' on my gal again, Sleeper, I'll geld you with one bullet."

The rifle muzzle lowered, and Monk took a hasty step backward. "Now, look — !"

"Get ridin'," Dunes said.

Monk hadn't expected to get off that easy and was soon in the saddle and riding down the slope, getting angrier with each step of the horse. Maybe the filly had been born by the white wife Dunes was said to have had before he came to the Wagonwheel, but a squaw had raised her. What made him think she was better than the other young squaws that'd meet a man in the sagebrush for some trinket? And how come a Sleeper was a particular red flag to Dunes?

Monk puzzled about that as he came out of the hills and angled toward the north fork of the Wildhorse, where the Big S had its headquarters at the foot of another range of hills. Once Monk had been with his father when they came on Dunes in the Van Bremer pass. The look that passed between the two men would have frozen hot lava, but his father hadn't explained when

Monk tried to find out what was back of it. After that, Monk was pretty sure that Purdy Sleeper feared Dunes.

Safely away from Forbidden Canyon, Monk began to feel like himself. The country he crossed was the floor of a curious basin at the tip of the great Shasta plateau. It was called the Wagonwheel because streams came out of several sets of encircling hills — the Coyote, Wildhorse, Lizard, Moccasin and Pistol — to flow into a lake in the center of the basin. It supported as many cattle and horse outfits as there were streams, if what Martin Dunes ran on the Coyote could be called a ranch.

Purdy Sleeper had taken up the last of the Wagonwheel three years ago, when Monk was nineteen, and so had got the poorest of it, to his continual dissatisfaction. He had the sometimes dry course of the north branch of Wildhorse Creek and wanted the south fork. Monk knew he also coveted the Coyote Hills, on the other side of Big S, which Dunes held but only used in small part. Yet if suspicion of that lay in Dunes' mind, it ought to be him afraid of Purdy and not the other way around.

When he came to Sentinel Peak, Monk stopped, dismounted and climbed to the top of the prominence, because he liked the sweeping view from there. The peak was an eroded lava cone that lifted him enough that he could see Hub Lake, where lived another filly he liked to lay his eyes on. The distance was too great for that now, but he could make out the four ranch headquarters along the south and east sides of the lake. Minto's, at the mouth of the South Wildhorse. Brown's and Trinkler's, on the west and east branches of Lizard Creek. Agee's, on the Moccasin, over at the east end of the lake. They had moved into the basin together, eight or ten years back, before it had been cleared of the Indians who had occupied it. By setting up their headquarters at the mouths of the creeks, they had been close enough to help protect each other from the Modocs, who were always jumping the reservation they had been moved to, up on Sprague River.

Monk's eyes ranged on toward Pistol Peak, off to the northeast and almost lost in the cold distance. Zack Buckman had his setup over there, running steers and raising horses. Zack was the one man in the Wagonwheel who could ride into Forbidden Canyon without wondering if he was about to get his head blown off. He was up at Tule Lake at present with the California Rifles, trying to root that blackhearted Indian Captain Jack out of the lava beds. Monk had seen him there that day without talking to him. They had never cottoned to each other, which seemed to suit both of them.

After descending to his horse, Monk mounted and cut a sharper slant to the west. The Big S headquarters were still lost in the wintry shadow of the Wildhorse Hills, but he rode unerringly toward them. A half hour later he came in

11

through a stand of juniper to a long, jerry-built cabin that stood in a cluster of half a dozen structures of like construction. Smoke wisped up from the cabin chimney, and he could tell by the corral that Purdy, Rip and Frank were all home. It was early for them to be there except now in deep winter, when there wasn't much to do outdoors.

He rode past the cabin, unsaddled his horse and turned it into the corral. When he stepped into the cabin, he found his father and two older brothers at the table, playing poker for beans. They had a jug on the table, Shasta dew that Rip had brought back from a visit to Yreka the previous week. They looked up at him, but nobody said anything immediately. Monk hung his hat and sheepskin on a wall peg, took off his gun rig and looped the belt over a chair back. He was the one who had been somewhere this time, and he enjoyed baffling their curiosity.

"Well," Purdy said impatiently, "what's doin' at the lake?"

"Gettin' set to go in after the Injuns," Monk said importantly.

"When?"

"Tomorrow."

"And," Rip said, "they're gonna get their tails shot off."

"They got a lot of army," Monk retorted. "Five cavalry companies and two volunteer out-fits from Oregon and the California Rifles. They moved to the bluffs over the lavas yesterday.

They got some cannons that come down from Fort Vancouver. That's what they've been waitin' for."

"Them Modocs," Rip said, "can shoot the teeth out of a gnat. On top of that, nobody goes breezin' into them lavas even without Injuns shootin' at 'em. I been in 'em, boy."

"You're right, Rip," Purdy said, and his eyes seemed to gleam. "Old Jack and them heathens of his're gonna be there quite a spell."

Monk couldn't see why they seemed to like that idea. Eighteen ranchers had been killed, scalped, gutted and emasculated while the Modocs, after licking some soldiers trying to herd them back to the reservation, had made their way to the stronghold in the lavas. The Wagonwheel had expected a similar fate until the army and militia companies arrived and sealed the Indians in the lavas. Or nearly sealed them. Plenty of them still slipped out to raid, and now and then somebody still lost his hair.

The Wagonwheel's worry stemmed from the fact that Hooker Jim, now one of the renegades, had been the chief of the little band that once had lived here. Dunes' squaw had been from that band, but Hooker had made his sentiments toward the rest of the white people known by leading the raid down the east side of Tule Lake that had resulted in the eighteen murders. And that wasn't country he had personally lost to the white stock ranchers.

"Then," Monk said, "there's gonna be some

blood spilled right here to home."

A curious look passed between his brothers; then they both glanced at Purdy, who had a smile on his mouth while he pretended to study his cards. If they thought the renegades would keep on endangering the country, why hadn't they joined up with John Fairchild's volunteers, like Zack Buckman, Ernie Yost and Bill Minto had? Monk had ached to enlist and get a crack at killing Indians. Not only had his father and brothers refrained from offering their services, but Purdy had put his foot down flat against Monk's doing it. Now Monk realized they had something in mind they still weren't letting him in on. It graveled him to be treated like a kid when he'd been of age over a year.

They finished the hand, and Frank prepared to deal again. "You want in, kid?" he asked.

Monk shook his head. He had never seen much sense in playing for beans. Money, property, or the women he'd heard of men gambling for made sense. But a man could win a whole sack of beans and have nothing but a windy belly.

He rolled a cigarette from Frank's tobacco, which lay on the table, puzzling on what made Purdy so happy if he expected the trouble to last. Nobody had a greater interest in the Wagonwheel, the whole Tule basin, for that matter. He was always talking about this range and that, its water and grass, like he made a close study of it. He often said there never could be more than five little outfits in the Wagon-wheel, while there could be one big one. He liked to say that a man who owned the Wagon-wheel could run the whole Tule. And that took in a lot of country — Dorris's spread on Hot Creek, Fairchild's on the Cottonwood, Van Bremer's on Willow Creek, and the outfits north and east of the lake that had been wiped out by the Modocs.

"How about us ridin' up there tomorrow," Monk suggested, "and watchin' the fireworks, at least?"

"We're stayin' out of it," Purdy snapped. "You, too."

Rip, a restless man, got tired of the game and threw in his hand. Frank got up to make the evening meal, since neither Rip nor Monk could cook very well and Purdy wouldn't. The jug had gone down a few inches since Monk got home, but none of them seemed drunk. A Sleeper could soak up a lot of liquor before it showed. Even Monk, although he liked to do his drinking in Yreka or Linkville or Winnemucca or Humboldt City, where there was reason for a man to get excited and get his nerve worked up. A reason like a woman. He could get randy as a buck rabbit just from spying on Wendy Dunes or Dora Agee, but he needed a few shots under his belt when it came to facing the hard-eyed, blunt-tongued jezebels hanging around the towns he knew.

He wished they hadn't left their Nevada ranch

in the Carson Valley, which had been within an easy ride of Virginia City and the other brawling camps on the big Comstock lode. Monk had grown up on that ranch and felt at home like he never had and maybe never would feel at home in the Wagonwheel. He still didn't see any sense in Purdy's making the long move north. The Carson spread had been small and hemmed in, but it had had more water and was only a skip and a jump from markets for the beef. The Sleepers hadn't got along with the neighbors, but then they didn't try to; nor did they here, either. It seemed to him that Purdy and the older sons went out of their way to make trouble with the Mintos, on the next creek.

Purdy used to talk continually about wanting a setup where a man could spread out in all directions, with range for as many steers as profits, rustling and bovine reproduction could give him. Finally he and Frank had ridden off on a trip that had taken them weeks. When they came back, Purdy had sold out, loaded the old wagon, rounded up the stock and hit the trail. Clear out of Nevada and nearly across the corner of California to the Oregon line. What Purdy saw in the arid Wildhorse country had been a mystery to Monk after he had arrived, and he had asked Frank, who was the oldest brother, what had decided Purdy on it.

"You tend to your growin' up, kid," Frank had said, "and leave men's work to men."

But they weren't treating him like a grownup

16

even yet, and Monk found himself scowling across the room at his father, who was idly watching Frank cook supper. All at once he thought of a way to make Purdy sit up and take notice.

"Come over the Coyotes on my way home," Monk said. "Stopped and talked a spell with Martin Dunes."

Purdy's long spine straightened. Rip looked up from a stick of pine he was whittling into a chain. At the stove Frank turned around, his face surprised and dark. Monk had expected that to get them. From what he had pieced together, Purdy, at least, had known Dunes elsewhere, and finding him here, holed up in Forbidden Canyon, was something he hadn't bargained for.

"It's that heifer," Frank drawled, "and she'll get him killed. You better tell him, Purdy."

"Tell me what?" Monk said when his father failed to say anything.

Purdy, strangely, had clenched his fists. He stopped staring at Monk and looked out the window. Then he turned his head again.

"What'd you talk about?" he said.

That was something Monk would never divulge. "The time of day. He asked where I'd been and I told him."

"You're lyin'. Martin Dunes wouldn't pass no time of day with us."

"Why not?"

"He don't like white folks."

"That won't keep this kid away from the girl," Frank said impatiently. "Dunes don't like us in particular, Monk. He blames Purdy for his white wife gettin' killed."

Monk stared at his father. "Where'd you know him?"

"Carson River," Purdy said with a hangdog look. "He lived there when you were a tyke. There was a little mistake over some horse stealin'. Some of us figured it was Dunes. He was a queer duck even then, sort of keepin' to himself. We went to get him, not figurin' to waste any more time on a horse thief than it took to knot a rope. Somebody shot at us from his cabin, and we all opened fire on it. Got in, and there was nobody there but his woman and little girl. Woman was dead. Shot. Dunes was off someplace. Guess we scared the woman, her alone, and she tried to shoo us off."

"Dunes been stealin' horses?"

Purdy sighed. "Not that time, anyhow. Next day they caught a different fella headin' for California with the missin' horses. Dunes left the country. Never knew what come of him till we got here."

"Sweet Jesus," Monk breathed. "No wonder you're scared of him, if he packs a grudge like that."

"Who said I'm scared of him?" Purdy said belligerently. But Monk knew he was, scared as hell. "Never tried to get even before he left the Carson, and he ain't tried here. So you never passed the time of day with him, and what did he say to you?"

"Never seen him," Monk lied. "Figured there was something between you and was only stirrin' it up."

"Well, you keep shy of there till he's salted down. No tellin' when he'll take it in his loco head to get even with me."

"Salted?" Monk said. "How?"

"Never mind how, but he will be. The Wagon-wheel ain't big enough for both of us, and I don't aim to leave."

CHAPTER II

A high bluff overlooked the lavas at the foot of Tule Lake, and, standing at its edge with his brother Del, Zack Buckman didn't know why so many worries wormed through his mind. Nearly everyone else in the big military camp, behind them on the bluff top, figured it would take only a few hours' fighting on the morrow to take care of the Modoc renegades hidden down there in that slag sea. Even Del, in the dusty field blue of the 1st Cavalry — Perry's company from Fort Warner — sergeant's stripes on his sleeves, had a lit-up look on his weathered face.

"What I keep wonderin'," Zack said moodily, "is how come none of the Sleepers joined up for this. Who likes shootin' up Injuns any better?"

"They're chicken-livered," Del said.

Zack shook his head. They both stood tall, men with wide shoulders and lean hips, young in years but seasoned a rocky hard by the frontier. Two years the older, Del had less than six months left to serve with the cavalry, after which he would come to the Wagonwheel to go partners on the stock ranch there. Zack's own loose-standing frame was clad in the worn range clothing that was regulation for Fairchild's California company of volunteers, six weeks in service now because of the Indian outbreak.

"The Sleepers' are a lot of things," Zack said, "but not yellow. I keep wonderin' if they're runnin' a private coon while this is goin' on."

He shook his head. His worry was hard to explain, even to Del, who understood him better than anybody else. Excepting the Sleepers, nearly every able-bodied man had left the Wagonwheel to offer his services after the bloody massacre in late November. Bill Minto was here, leaving his crippled brother Johnny home to run the spread in the Wildhorse Hills at a time when the relationship between the Sleepers and Mintos was an outright hill-country feud. Ernie Yost, who worked for Hollis Brown, was also here. That left only three men to defend themselves, and the balance of the Wagonwheel, if the Sleeper clan was up to dirty work. Martin Dunes would stay out of it, Zack figured, its being Dunes' idea that the country had received its quota of whites when he and Wendy moved there, years ahead of anybody else.

Old Purdy was range-hungry, and his muscular offspring were trouble-hungry, with the oversized kid, Monk, horny as a young bull but lacking even a bull's natural restraints. It had been several months since Zack caught onto the fact that Monk was stalking Wendy Dunes, would be capable of almost anything if he got hold of her. And his suspicion was mounting that Purdy saw in the Indian trouble something he had been hunting for ever since he moved into the Wagonwheel.

"Well," Del was saying, "this'll be over in a day or two, and you can get back there."

"What if it's not?" Zack retorted. "Goin' into the lavas won't be a surrey ride. The Modocs're apt to be somewhere else, even if we can beat our way into that stronghold of theirs. So we could be held in the militia a long while yet. With the Sleepers foxes in the hen house down there."

Del was frowning now. His life was still the cavalry, but he already had a stake in the Wagonwheel much larger than his interest in the coming partnership. Of even greater importance, Zack knew, was the redheaded girl on the next creek, Dora Agee, whom Del had met once while there on a furlough. The two had taken to each other right off.

"When bloodthirsty hombres keep out of a fight," Del conceded, "they've got a good reason. But I think we'll get this Injun trouble settled now. The general's got four hundred troops, and there's only supposed to be fifty-sixty warriors in there with Jack."

"I sure hope you're right."

It had been Zack who worked on the Texas cattle trail while Del tried a hitch in the cavalry, who found and fell in love with the rugged sage-rock-juniper plateau lying in the north-eastern shadow of towering Mount Shasta. It had originally belonged to the Modocs, but a treaty with them nearly ten years back had resulted in their being moved to the Klamath reservation. That had let white stockmen, who had grazed the country on a migratory basis before, take up permanent ranches, and men like Press Dorris and John Fairchild and a score of others had taken over in the lake country.

The trouble was, the Klamaths and Modocs had been enemies much longer than the Modocs had hated the white people. Cooped up on the same reserve and badly outnumbered, the Modocs had come in for abuse and rough treatment from the Klamaths. Some of them, under Captain Jack, had jumped twice now and come back to their old country. The first time they had let themselves be talked into returning to the reservation, where the improvements promised were not made. This time Jack didn't mean to go back unless it was with his toes pointed up.

Zack didn't blame them for loving this country. From where he stood with Del he could, if he had field glasses, see nearly all of it on this cold, clear day of mid-January. With the naked eye he could make out the range of mountains to the south that divided the Modoc and Pit River countries. That was where the Wagonwheel lay, lost beyond the low mountains. Ranging north was the vast basin of Tule Lake, most conspicuously marked by the lake and the lavas below it, ejected in the long ago by Mount Shasta. The lake, a sagebrush sea, was eleven miles each way at its widest. The billowing slag on the south end was three or four miles narrower but extended nearly to the Wagonwheel.

The lavas thinned to the south and contained, down there, many small meadows of bunch grass, where, more than once, Zack and his neighbors had had to hunt stray stock.

Directly out from the army camp on top of the bluff, and beyond the sweep of rock waste, was the outpost of Captain Bernard's cavalry company from Fort Bidwell, there in a not too successful effort to hold the Indians in their stronghold and stop their murderous raids in the basin. On the far shore of the lake, above Bernard's camp, were the deserted ranches where so many mutilated bodies had been found after the renegades, under Hooker Jim, came scorching down from Lost River to take refuge in the lavas. North of there was Bloody Point, scene of the massacre of a wagon company bound for the mines in California. At the upper end of the lake, where Lost River fed in its water, the Modocs had written yet another chapter in their bloody rebellion against white rule.

The camps of Hooker Jim and Captain Jack had stood there after the second break from the reservation, one on either side of the river. There in late November had arrived Odeneal, the Indian Superintendent, with Captain Jackson and thirty-five cavalrymen from Fort Klamath. Their mission was to talk the renegades back onto the reservation or force them, with their minds leaning to the latter course. In the fight, which anybody who knew these particular Modocs could have predicted, several soldiers had been killed outright, with a dozen wounded fatally, without a loss to the Indians. Leaving the scene, Jack had come down the west side of the lake to hole up in the lavas. Hooker Jim, moving down the east side, showed a nature much different from Jack's, leaving behind among the dead eighteen white men. For a time the Wagonwheel had expected the same fate, which it could still experience if this trouble wasn't settled on the morrow. It was Hooker's old home range, just as Jack's had been on Lost River. . . .

Jarred from his thoughts by Del's voice, Zack looked at his brother. "Reckon I better get back to the company," Del was saying. "That damned looey's bound to run some more practice charges before dark."

Zack grinned. The main army base had been established at Van Bremer's ranch on Willow Creek, about a dozen miles to the west. Two days ago the troops had been issued three days' rations and, in light marching order, had struck off across an exceedingly rough country of ridges and slopes to this position; the supply train had had to take a more roundabout way. After reaching the bluff at noon, the command had been put through a series of drills, practice marches and fake charges that had lasted that day and through the next. The Modocs, who beyond question had spied on them from some rocky elevation, must have wondered what invisible enemy they were attacking with such energy.

Del had offered his hand, and Zack took it

with a tightening in his chest. "See you after, if not during, the rumpus," Del said lightly, and started off toward the bluecoat section of the camp. But would they see each other then? Zack had a bleak wonder as to what was in the cards for them. The dice were in the cup, and it remained to be seen whether they would ever run the ranch together the way they had dreamed.

For a moment before he started for the volunteers' camp, Zack took a look at the force assembled to penetrate the lavas and restore peace and security to the Tule country. The militia camp, which bivouacked the California company — now officially mustered into the federal service and on its payroll — and two more from Oregon, lay south of the regular cavalry.

The volunteers, totaling a hundred and fifty men, were a motley aggregation, lacking in military spit and polish but not in *esprit de corps*. Most of the members came from the mining centers to the west — Yreka, Jacksonville and the camps around them. While they were mainly without experience in fighting the desert Indians, they had chosen seasoned leaders. John Fairchild, who had been elected captain of the California outfit, had a stock ranch off there to the west, close to Van Bremer's. The Oregon militia was commanded by John Ross of Jacksonville, who had fought Rogue Indians through the five-year war with them. Its companies were captained by Harrison Kelly and Oliver Applegate, seasoned frontiersmen.

The cavalry encampment was not only much more smartly military but also larger, totaling over two hundred men, with another fifty east at Bernard's outpost. These were from the regular army posts in the region — a company of the 1st from Fort Klamath under Jackson, who had already felt Modoc claws at the mouth of Lost River; Perry's company from Fort Warner, to which Del belonged; Adams' from Fort Harney; and Mason's from Fort Bidwell. In command of both regulars and militia was Colonel Frank Wheaton, a brevet general from the Civil War who still enjoyed that rank as a courtesy title and whose regular headquarters were at Warner.

The plan of attack had been explained and discussed at even greater length by the men than by the general and his officers. Colonel John Green, in command at Fort Klamath, would lead the assault on the west side of the lavas while Bernard moved in from the east flank. Once penetration of the lavas was achieved, the two skirmish lines would wheel so as to bring their south flanks together, thereupon driving north and pinning the Modocs against the lake. After that it would be like killing rabbits in a surround, most of the men maintained.

The bluecoats had mess tents, cooks and KPs, but the volunteers rustled their own grub, forming into messes of a few men each. Zack had thrown in with the other two men from the Wagonwheel, whom he found smoking by the

27

dying supper fire. Bill Minto, tall, dark and craggy, gave him a somber nod, and Zack knew his thoughts also were troubled, not only by the coming day, but also by concern for his stiff-kneed brother, who was holding down the spread back home in the Wildhorse Hills.

Ernie Yost was a half-pint, irrepressibly gay, even though he was no stranger to hardship and danger. Yost said with a grin, "Them lavas look any easier than when I seen 'em this afternoon?"

"They don't show much improvement," Zack said.

"They'll show even less tomorrow," Yost said, sobering. "You ought to have heard what Fairchild told some of the Injun-eaters a while ago. Said he's worried about holdin' 'em back after they smell Modocs. Back, that is, from climbin' the bluff and gettin' the hell outta there. And speakin' of John, there he is."

John Fairchild was coming toward them from the bluecoat camp, a sandy-haired man with steel-gray eyes under thick eyebrows. He and Press Dorris had been among the first to come into the lake country, and they had built up big outfits on Cottonwood and Hot creeks. Over in their neighborhood there had been a band of peaceful Modocs, in no way connected with Jack's renegades. The two ranchers not only treated them well but paid grazing fees for such of their land as they used for their stock. Since the Hot Creeks, as these Indians were called, were entirely amiable in disposition, they had

28

not been forced to move to the reservation.

But after Hooker Jim's bloody raid and the bitterness it had engendered among the white people, Fairchild had deemed it advisable for the Hot Creeks to go to the reservation voluntarily until Jack's band had been dealt with. He had guaranteed them safe-conduct, and the Hot Creeks had agreed. So Fairchild had sent word to the agent at the reservation, asking him to meet these Indians with a cavalry escort at the Klamath ferry, a short distance north of Lower Klamath Lake.

In spite of Fairchild's care, word of his plan had reached Linkville, which had been up in arms over the massacre. When Fairchild and Dorris had reached the ferry with their charges they had been met not by the Indian agent and cavalry escort but by an inflamed mob from Linkville resolved to hang the Hot Creeks. The two ranchers had stood off this horde with fisted pistols and hot tongues, cowing its leaders and forcing the mob to withdraw. But when they had finally been able to turn their attention back to their charges, the Hot Creeks had vanished. Only later had the ranchers learned that, feeling themselves betrayed, the Hot Creeks had cut a beeline for the lavas, adding fourteen warriors to the fifty already there under Captain Jack. Shacknasty Jim and Steamboat Frank were two of them, good Indians ordinarily but hell on wheels once their blood was hot. . . .

Fairchild came up to his company, which was

no more inclined to show him a stiff military respect than he was of a disposition to want it. To the loungers he said, "On your feet, boys. We're goin' over to the commissary and draw what we need for tomorrow. A hundred rounds apiece, and grub for the noon meal."

"It's gonna take us that long, John?" Yost asked. "Clean till noon to clean a handful of Injuns *outta them lavas?*"

Fairchild, knowing he was ribbing the fire-breathing element from the mining camps, grinned at him. "Oughtn't to take that long, Ernie. But the general thought it'd be nice to have a picnic lunch in there afterwards."

The company got languidly to its feet and followed him off across the thin, rocky soil of the bluff top to the cavalry encampment. By the time the men got back to their own camp, night had rolled in over the desert. Sagebrush fires were built higher against the increasing chill. Laughter mixed with the smoke, and from here and there came the sound of harmonicas.

CHAPTER III

Not far to the east, in the heart of the lavas, no one had been allowed or cared to seek the comfort of his blankets. This center of resistance was a huge craterlike depression in the vast field of rock, its only life that which had been forced to seek refuge there, its internal water only that left in natural cisterns by the rains. In the caves indenting the walls of the depression were the Modoc families. Sixty-four of their number were effective warriors; several times that number were noncombatants.

This was the stronghold proper, a hub whose spokes ran out as trails to many parts of the lava beds. To the bluffs on the west, where scouts that day had watched the huge force of "Boston" soldiers prepare to kill Modocs. To the east, where there was a smaller encampment of white soldiers. To the south and the grassy pockets in the lavas, where stolen beef cattle and horses could be kept. And north to the lake, about three-quarters of a mile away through a deep trench that ensured a water supply after the cisterns dried up in late spring.

In concentric rings for some distance around the stronghold were defense outposts, fortified by rocky breastworks, connected by natural trenches and tubes that made it a fortress without equal. On the wide perimeter beyond these fortifications were miles of volcanic terrain, against which an invader could wear himself to exhaustion before he came in reach of a Modoc target.

In the stronghold and out on the breastworks, as the night drew deeper and colder, some of the Modoc women and striplings, keenly alert, manned the watches. Others brought sagebrush for the fires or molded lead into bullets for the rifles, while the warriors and wise old men gathered around a fire in the depression's open center.

They were a hybrid lot. For twenty years, in more peaceful times, they had mingled with the white people in the mining centers under Mount Shasta — Yreka, Hawkinsville, Humbug and a dozen others. Many of them had worked as servants in white homes, and some of the women had lived with miners. About half of those squatted around the council fire wore "Boston" clothes and spoke a rough version of the white man's language. In the years in which they had mingled with the white people, they had got so used to this tongue that they often used it among themselves. They had so long answered to the names the white men had bestowed on them that they had also adopted them: Captain Jack, Scarface Charley, Boston Charley, Bogus Charley, Black Jim, Hooker Jim, Shacknasty Jim, Curly Doctor.

Although he had led this band from the time

it turned renegade, Captain Jack sat by the sage fire almost as an impassive spectator. He was an ugly man, stocky, twisted, his skin Negroid in color, his glistening black hair whacked short and ragged. No descendant of chiefs, he had risen to leadership by acclamation, a fact that had engendered resentments in a few men in his splinter band of Modocs. At last he rose and silently searched the shadow-flicked countenances they turned toward him. He doubted that a third of them would accord with the feelings so weighing on his heart. Of his headmen, he knew he could count only on tough Scarface Charley for loyalty to the bitter end.

After a long moment of silence, Jack began to speak in the tribal tongue: "In the snows that have come since old Schonchin led many Modocs in this country" — he nodded at Schonchin John, the old chief's jealous brother, in a gesture of conciliation — "we have killed many white men. Yet more have come. We cannot kill all of them. They are like the grass and trees and stars. There is no end to them. We are not afraid to die, for we are Modocs. But when we die, there is no one to take our place."

Jack saw the scowls draw deeper on the tight countenances the firelight showed him. He lifted a hand.

"Listen, my people. I speak with a straight tongue. Our people, most of them, are on the reservation. There old Schonchin still leads them. They bear the abuses of the Klamaths.

33

They try to believe the lies of the agents, no matter how many promises have not been kept. We have tried that. Twice we believed the peace men they sent us and went to the reservation. But we could not keep on believing when we learned they spoke with forked tongues. When the peace man came with soldiers to make us go to the reservation again, we made war."

A growl went around the circle of listeners. They had merely shot Jackson's command to pieces in the fight at Lost River, without a loss to themselves. Again Jack lifted a hand against the vainglorious pride he saw swell in so many of them, and he shook his ragged head.

"Hear me speak. Tomorrow we must make war again, or tonight we must make peace. I do not know if we can make peace. But we are few and they are many. My heart tells me that before we make war we must send word to the white chief that we want to talk with him."

The instant Jack sat down, Schonchin John boiled to his feet, his sharp face twisted in fury. Before he could launch into a raging protest, Curly Doctor, the medicine man, was up and shouting. Hooker Jim drowned him out to remind Jack that surrender meant the prompt hanging of himself and the warriors who had ridden with him in the recent massacre, a good half of those there.

Scarface Charley, who had the voice of a bull, shouted them all down.

"You have heard our chief," he said in the

sudden quiet, "and he speaks true. When we came to the rocks, we thought we had only the ranchers and a few soldiers to fight. We knew we could fight them and make them let us live here in peace. But now they have brought more soldiers than we can count. Maybe they cannot come in and kill us or drive us out of the rocks. But they can make us stay here and starve to death or die because we have no water. Kientepoos —" He looked at Jack, whose Indian name he had used. "Kientepoos has this on his heart. It is heavy. We must do what he says."

Scarface went on to point out that their chief had no thought of an abject surrender. They were in a strong bargaining position, for they could make it costly for the white soldiers, no matter what the outcome of a war. Jack would exact a price, demanding amnesty for the crimes, real or imagined, charged against the Modocs. He would demand the reservation on Lost River once promised them, with guarantees that this time they would get it and be allowed to keep it. No harm could come from trying to negotiate with the white chief out of such strength. If he failed, then there would be war.

When Scarface finished speaking, Curly Doctor got to his feet, his rise continuing the hush in the rest. In addition to being a clever politician, he wielded an enormous superstitious power over the band. He spoke in scorn of any further agreements made with the white men, whose outcome had already been demonstrated by the broken promises of the past. Surrender meant death, to which a fighting death was vastly preferable to a Modoc. But there would be no death either way. Curly Doctor would make medicine that would turn away the white men's bullets and help the Modocs kill the soldiers. Kamoocumchux, the Great Spirit, was stronger than all the white armies, and Curly Doctor's influence with him was great.

At the shout of approval that followed this impassioned harangue, Jack admitted his defeat. He ordered that the question be settled by vote, those favoring war to line up with Curly Doctor and Schonchin John, its strongest advocates. Those who wanted to ask for a parley were to join himself and Scarface Charley.

His earlier estimate had been accurate. Fourteen warriors fell in with him, nearly fifty gathered around his opposers. It was war. So be it. He was their chief, and he would do his best to lead them through whatever lay ahead.

Jack swung away from the council and went toward his cave, hearing behind him the preparations for a war dance. Already the fire burned higher, an electric excitement charging the air. From other caves poured women, for theirs was an important part in the ceremony; and the old men came forth behind the women; and then came the children. Jack's heart swelled in spite of his misgivings, for they were truly a brave people. The blood of warriors flowed strong in all their veins.

The fire had grown bright enough to bring his own cave into illumination. As he stepped in, Jack saw that his family had listened intently to the proceedings in which he had lost his case. He looked at them, his old wife now worn and reduced to the status of servant in favor of the young wife, Lizzie, he had taken. He glanced at his sister, whom the whites called Queen Mary because of her fine carriage. There was the handsome daughter by the old wife, now eighteen, and the darling of his heart by the young wife, now three. He regarded them sternly, none of his deep affection showing, causing them to lower their eyes.

But when he had seated himself on his blankets, he spoke with kindness. "I'll watch out for the little one. Go and watch."

The eyes of the women were grateful when they left. Only when he was alone with the baby girl did the chief let the stolid set of his face relax and reveal the troubledness it had concealed.

He put more faith in his own foresight than in Curly Doctor's influence with Kamoocumchux. Thanks to that faculty, and a good people to lead, the stronghold was well stocked from raids on the ranches of Langell and Poe valleys and those encircling the basin lakes. There were large numbers of stolen horses and cattle in the hidden meadows of the lavas, meaning food for a long time. There were sufficient firearms and ammunition to last a great while if used carefully, some of it taken from the ranches, the rest in a way that still made his heart swell with pride.

The arrival of the military forces east and west of the stronghold had been followed by a great deal of wagon freighting from Fort Bidwell and the railroad in Nevada over the old emigrant road from the east. After the hole-up and a few days before the white people's Christmas, Modoc warriors had intercepted one of these shipments within earshot of Captain Bernard's outpost at the southeast corner of the lake. The train had been escorted by six soldiers, all of whom, with five of the horses, fell under the hail of Indian lead that greeted them from trailside rocks. The shots had been heard in the army camp. But before Bernard could rush help to his wagons, the Indians got away with the ammunition the wagons had been carrying to help kill Modocs.

Half a moon later, even to the Modocs' surprise, the soldiers let themselves be caught again in the same situation and at almost the same place. This time the teamster, who escaped the first storm of bullets, whipped up his teams and went careening down the trail toward the army camp. While he and the soldier escort escaped with their lives, most of the load was jolted out of the wagons and scattered behind. Along with more ammunition, the Indians came into possession of a keg of whisky. That night they built a huge fire on a prominence within sight of the army camp and put on a victory dance. Jack liked to think of what had been in the minds of the soldiers who watched.

Yet he knew the future would not hold many more such incidents. Food and ammunition could be stretched, sometimes unbelievably, yet only so far. Raiding for more would be costly, if not impossible, with so many yellowlegs about. The cistern water would vanish with the heat of summer, after which the Modocs, if they still held out, would be dependent on the lake. The trail to the lake, although well protected and easy to defend, would become their jugular vein. If cut, it would be the end, and the white war chief would be smart enough to concentrate on cutting it.

Jack could tell by the sounds coming into the cave how far the war dance had progressed. By now the fanatic Curly Doctor was in his cave, preparing the food and herbs he would present to Kamoocumchux. Even as Jack keened his ears, he heard the gaunt Indian call to the women to freshen the ceremonial fire they had built, on which the offerings would be made. Jack rose and went to the cave entrance just as the medicine man came out to the ceremonial fire and began to place the offerings on the red coals to convert them to a form in which the Great Spirit could consume them.

Meanwhile Curly Doctor chanted shrill, rhythmic incantations, the women accompanying him, their voices pitched by nature to the high key of the medicine man. Somewhere a drummer began to beat on a dried rawhide drum, causing the women to sway their hips and twist their bodies. Then the women began their dance of supplication, their movements irregular, swaying, hopping, twisting, their faces contorted as they pleaded for the immunity Curly Doctor had promised from the soldiers' bullets. The warriors, excluded from the performance, stood watching with glistening eyes. The old and young, standing back of them, began to sway from the influence of the frenzy growing in the dancers.

Jack turned impatiently away, a troubled man spiritually, not sure what powers lay behind the brutal, detectable forces that ruled life on earth. After returning to his blankets, he sat motionless as the weird rock of the lavas while the war dance reached its climax and abruptly ended.

His mind had gone back two decades to a summer when Kientepoos had been a stripling and Modocs had lived in all the beautiful valleys of Lost River. That was the time of the wagons with the white sails, hordes of them coming out of the east and crossing Modoc country to what Kientepoos later learned were the new gold mines in California.

It befell that summer that the Pit Indians, a troublesome tribe that lived over the ranges to the south, stole some horses from settlers living near the new white men's town of Yreka. And out of Yreka came a horde of miners to open a surprise attack on a Modoc village in which women, children and old ones fell with the warriors. Protestations of innocence made no difference, for to the miners one Indian was like another and one's guilt was shared by all.

So it followed that the Modocs applied the white men's rule, falling upon the next wagon train and killing everyone in it, some forty people. In consequence there came another company of citizen-soldiers, led by Ben Wright, but not as warriors. They came, said Wright, to make peace and establish friendship, and he caused a great feast to be prepared, to which he invited the Modocs, insisting only that they leave their weapons outside of camp. But before the feast began, Wright's men, on signal, caught up hidden firearms and opened up on the astonished Modocs. There had been nearly forty of them, and only four escaped alive. Kientepoos had been one of these, old Schonchin another.

The Modocs had never forgiven that, but they had tried to forget it. They made no more trouble and were left alone, and Kientepoos grew to manhood. By then there was mingling between the races, and some of the Modoc women went with white men to be their squaws, and the young bucks found themselves drawn to the excitement of the Shasta camps. Kientepoos, too, often made long stays at Yreka, where his sister Mary and cousin Winema had gone to live with white husbands. And he had found a special friend in Elija Steele, a Yreka lawyer who acted as Indian agent for northern California. Steele had been the first white man to affirm the Modocs' perpetual right to the land in the Tule basin.

The trouble was that Lost River, the best part of this region, ran in a great horseshoe bend out of Clear Lake to the east before emptying into Tule Lake, with its bending central lengths crossing into Oregon. Therefore, said the Oregon Indian superintendent, Steele had no authority and the Modocs must move to the reservation set up in south-central Oregon for the Klamaths. The upshot was the two reservation breaks on which Kientepoos had led his splinter faction. And to what end — death in the lavas?

Now, with the fatal decision so near, Jack was less confident of his course than he had been in more defiant days in the past. But his people had chosen, and if he did not act as their war chief, as he had been their peace chief, that role would be filled by Schonchin John or Curly Doctor. Jack distrusted their wisdom, even their motives, and knew that, come what may, theirs would be a bloodier leadership than his.

It had grown quiet in the camp, Jack realized. At last he rolled up in his blankets for a little sleep.

Somewhere toward dawn a hand on his shoulder awakened him. The central fire still burned to warm those obliged to remain awake. By its light Jack saw the face of Scarface Charley over him, a face ugly as his own, with the slashing indentation of an old wound drawn across his right cheekbone.

"Kientepoos," Charley whispered. "Look — out there."

Jack blinked drowsy eyes and grew aware of an unnaturalness in the atmosphere. There was a heaviness in the air itself. Then he rose and hurried to the cave entrance to stare into a dense fog that in the early hours of morning had descended over the lavas. It had seeped even into the depression occupied by the Modocs.

Jack regarded it in amazement, then turned his head to look at his one trusted lieutenant. Curly Doctor had made good his boasts. His medicine was indeed strong.

CHAPTER IV

No bugle rang over the bluffs above the lava beds, where sprawled the military encampment. Bluecoats and volunteers came awake at the touches or quiet voices of the noncoms, torn from uneasy dreams. By the light of the morning star and its paler sister planets, they tugged on boots and hats. They were quiet, too. This was the day — January 17, 1873 — that might well be engraved on the headstones of some, maybe quite a few of them.

At the mess tents coffee stood ready, steaming in the chilly air beside stacks of hardtack round and tough as flapjacks cured in a tanning vat. The militia ate with the regulars for once, to save time. Even so, the command scarcely had knocked the edge off its appetite when the order came to fall in for muster. Then John Fairchild strode away to report his California company present and ready for action. The Oregon captains, Applegate and Kelly, were doing the same. Zack looked around at a strangely hushed group left behind, each man now wearing a cartridge belt furnished by the army and carrying rations for one meal somewhere on his person.

Ernie Yost had his hat pushed to the back of his head and held his rifle in a careless grip across his shoulders, a little bravado in his bearing to fool anyone who might suspect his nervousness. Bill Minto had tightened his face to an inscrutable hardness, and he met Zack's glance with dull impassivity. Off across the cindery space between the camps the regulars, smartly aligned, were still barking responses to muster. Perry's company was at the west end, but Zack could not be sure, at the distance and in that light, that Del was the sergeant ticking off the roll call.

Ernie Yost said, "Them cavalry must feel lost without their nags. Wonder how they're gonna like tradin' sore hind ends for sore feet?"

A man beyond him said, "If that's all that's sore, come night, they'll like it fine, I reckon."

At his tent Frank Wheaton, colonel of the 1st Cavalry Regiment, stood with Ross of the Oregon militia and Colonel John Green, who was to command the day's operation. With a glance at the stars, Wheaton spoke with easy confidence.

"Looks like we'll have a good day for it. I was worried about it being clear enough for Bernard to read our signals from his side of the beds."

"Luck seems to be with us, sir," the colonel agreed. "It's going to be clear as a bell."

"Take them in, then," Wheaton said, and offered his hand.

Orders crackled through the command. The volunteers, of better acquaintance with the vicinity, moved out first: Applegate, Kelly and then Fairchild. Zack cuffed Bill Minto on the arm, then turned to follow Yost off across the cinders. He was glad Del's company was just behind them. He saw that the early streaks of dawn were in the sky beyond the lavas. They moved briskly for a moment; then the whole line came to a stop.

Oliver Applegate and his sixty hushed frontiersmen had reached the edge of the bluff to see in the strengthening light what lay below on the lavas and over the whole basin floor — fog, dense, damp, and so deep nothing showed but a few lava peaks. Applegate had called a halt where a narrow, steep, and treacherous shelf trail dropped to the lower level.

When Green rushed up to see what had caused the hitch, he found himself confronted, at the very outset of his operation, by a staggering problem. Having served some time at Fort Klamath, he was no stranger to these sudden, low-lying plateau fogs that might last an hour or all day. There below was one that thoroughly scrambled the careful plans Wheaton and his staff had prepared. Yet at his level Green could see all the way to the deceptive, now-fading stars.

The colonel was in a quandary. Not only would the fog hide the sharpshooting Modocs out there in the fog-drowned rocks, but it would make it hard to keep the command in any kind of cohesion. It had rendered useless the howitzers with which he had expected to shell the stronghold later in the attack. He had lost his means of communicating with Bernard by signal flags and heliograph.

The responsible thing would be to postpone the attack until the fog lifted, but Bernard also had orders to attack at daylight. Neither Green nor Bernard could be sure that the other had not done so regardless of the fog, and if either delayed it might leave the other unsupported. The only way dispatch bearers could communicate between the commands was by a detour of the lavas, a ride of several hours, with the light above the fog already growing strong.

Green knew that Bernard was wrestling with the same dilemma and would have to reach the same conclusion. Neither being sure the other would delay, both had to move in on schedule regardless of complications.

"Proceed with your men, Captain," Green told Applegate.

Applegate's volunteers looked at each other, and taut faces grew tighter while again the men moved out, single file, disappearing figure by figure over the brink, the point probing its way down the tricky trail to the bottom. By the time Zack found himself on the descending shelf, part of the point had vanished into the sea of vapor. The ground below the bluff was open and fairly level for some distance. Applegate led his company left, toward the lake. The California company followed, Yost's figure ahead of Zack and Minto's, behind, turned spectral by the swirling mists.

Presently they halted and began what seemed an endless wait while the other companies came down, were swallowed, the last half turning right and away from the lake. By the time they were all down, the skirmish line stretched for three-fifths of a mile. No one in it could distinguish an object beyond fifty yards. Zack felt his nerves growing ever tighter. Miles of this blinded, hellish terrain lay between them and the stronghold proper, and Bernard's command had to cross only a slightly narrower stretch of it. And the penetration and juncture had to be made before the main assault could even be launched.

Zack wished they would get at it, but they only waited in the chill, damp obscurity, the command "Keep contact" going continually along the line, but with nobody moving enough to risk losing it. Time and again he strained his eyes while he looked to the right, dimly seeing the near end of Perry's company but unable to make out Del anywhere over there.

"Gonna be time to eat our rations pretty soon," Yost grumbled.

The stealth practiced to that point had been meant to let Green advance his men over the rocks as far as possible before the Modoc outposts could be sure an attack impended. Now the colonel needed to move his men as a unit. When he was sure his skirmish line was formed and intact, he gave the command to move forward. Bugles, fog-muted but carrying, transmitted the order to the ends of the line.

The command moved briskly and evenly across the band of level ground between the bluff and beds. It was impossible to judge distance, but it seemed to Zack they had advanced quite a way before the ground abruptly grew broken enough to slow parts of the line. A few minutes later the line was broken in two without its being immediately discovered. The result was a long wait and milling in the fog while the severed ends were reunited.

Thereafter the ground grew ever more broken, the advance, still unchallenged, slower and slower. Sometimes the obstruction would be a deep natural trench into which part of the line stumbled and fell, other times a ridge to be climbed, a chimney to move around. The word crackled along the line to halt, to hurry, and in spite of that there were maddening lags and dangerous salients began to form ahead.

Still the fog had not been jarred by a single shot.

But there was bleeding. As the stumbling, bumbling, sometimes crawling troops slid into a depression or climbed over an elevation, the sharp rocks cut their hands, their boots, their clothes. Now and then someone skinned an elbow or knee or twisted an ankle, but there was no turning back even for the injured. But the command kept moving, closer and closer to the stronghold, which began to figure in their imaginations as the innermost compartment of hell. The halts for straightening the line grew more frequent, lasted longer.

"This ain't no war," Yost complained. "It's blindman's buff in a rock quarry."

And then they heard the sound they had awaited with mixed dread and hope; it was about eight o'clock, some two hours after entering the beds. Although the fog nearly reduced it to inaudibility, there came from ahead of them a low, crackling and angry sound. Excitement rippled instantly along the ragged line. Green had made no mistake in driving the unit into the lavas. Bernard's command was advancing toward it and, somewhere out in the shrouded mystery, had made contact with the Modocs.

This awareness pumped new energy into Green's command, and it had moved another hundred yards when a daub of red dissolved the grayness ahead. The sound of the rifle producing it drilled through the fog, and over on Kelly's line a man jerked upright, threw back his head and fell. His flankers turned to help him, moving instinctively, only to have a dozen guns cut loose at them from the forward fog. One of the would-be helpers fell across the hurt man, himself hit. The other cut for the nearest cover.

"It's a war all right," Yost admitted, bug-eyed.

But an eerie one, for nobody could see far enough to fix the place from which the shots had come. Yet the Modocs had seen them, and this increased the confusion all along the line, which staggered, wavered, then steadied when

50

the bugle rapped quick commands.

"Return fire!"

And then: "Charge!"

The ringing notes reminded the men that there was still plan and purpose here, that Bernard's command was close enough to be heard, although nobody knew how far the sound of mass shooting would carry over a multisurfaced rock sounding board in a dense fog. The two units could now join, wheel, and begin to hammer the Modocs against the lake. The men went forward with a shout, the glaze of gun muzzles a leaping wildfire in the blanket of mist, the percussion rebounding from a thousand rocks and yet losing its sharpness in the dense, now smoke-thickened atmosphere.

But the ground ahead began to rise. Men tripped and fell headlong, the sharp rocks leaving long, bleeding cuts. Those little red sunbursts ahead skipped back and forth, and Zack shot at each one he saw, and more than once he felt the heat of a bullet fan his face. He knew men were going down all along the volunteer sector. Once when he flung a look to the right he could see nothing at all of Perry's company and wondered if the volunteers had outrun the main line.

The Modocs seemed to have been retreating, putting up a waspish rear-guard action, but all at once they stopped and began to whack in a furious fire. Other Indians had joined them, Zack realized. The command had come to the fortified perimeter of the stronghold, where the Modocs had the advantage of short, interior lines and fought from strong, carefully prepared positions. A moment later the companies of Applegate, Kelly and Fairchild were pinned down, contact with the regulars was lost.

Ernie Yost crawled over to Zack. There was sweat on his face in spite of the chilling fog. Now that the line had stopped moving, the smell of burned powder was a heavy, dampish stench.

Yost wiped the back of his hand across his nostrils and said, "I've come within a hair of my everlastin' half a dozen times. And damn me if I've caught a glimpse of a redskin. How come they can see us?"

Zack had puzzled over the same question. If they had killed any Indians, it was only because of a saturating fire poured in their direction. He knew the volunteers alone had suffered heavy losses, without the Modocs seeming to do a tenth as much shooting. It was uncanny.

No one on the line could fathom the secret of savage eyes somehow sharper than his own, of aims surer, although to that point the volunteers on the north flank had borne the brunt of the Indian counterfire. At the center of the line with his aide-de-camp and bugler, Green knew there was not a cavalry company either that had not lost men covering the last hundred yards. The fire bristling out of the fog was soon so heavy that his troops could do nothing but take cover and try to fire back. He hadn't the faintest notion of how far he had yet to advance before wheeling to make the flank connection with Bernard.

And there the battle froze through the rest of the morning. The Modocs were done with yielding ground, and from behind their breastworks of piled lava rock or out of natural trenches or from the elevation of some fumarole they erected a bullet barrier between the "Boston" soldiers and their stronghold. At eleven o'clock Green knew the operation was dangerously behind schedule. The lieutenant he had sent off through the fog in an attempt to contact Bernard had not come back.

Just before noon Green shifted his companies so that those who had been in the heaviest of the fighting could be spelled by those who had come off easier. Fairchild's volunteers were put on the north flank for an anchor, Kelly's went next to them, and Perry's regulars were swung in between Kelly and Applegate. The fog still smothered the lavas, and Green reconciled himself to the prospect of its not raising at all that day.

Yet how could he hope to achieve a victory if it did not? The only chance, and not a good one, was another attack on whatever lay hidden ahead of him, driving on until Bernard was contacted. He urged the weary line forward again, and, somewhat to his surprise, it could move, the underfooting worsening, the Indian sharpshooters resisting yet falling back. The command lost heavily again, yet it inched forward until, in midafternoon, a sudden high ridge of sharp, solid lava stopped it cold again. The Indians, under pressure, had fallen back to it. Now, from its summit, they made a new, unyielding stand. There still was no juncture with Bernard, no sign of him.

Again and again Green threw his men against the ridge, a frightful prominence of glass-sharp rock that shredded even the boots of the men. Each charge he called for was delivered bravely and bloodily. After the third, Green called it off and ordered the bugler to sound officers' call.

It took a while for the company commanders to reach the command post. While they hunkered behind a rock chimney, Green admitted frankly that he was stumped.

"They're concentrating on their right flank," he told his officers. "This ridge helps them hold this end. I expect their big worry's being cut off from the lake and the water they'll have to get from there later in the season."

"They're doin' a right good job of holdin' on to it, too," Fairchild commented.

Green nodded his complete agreement. "It seems to me our best chance for a quick decision is to hit them on that flank with everything we can throw at it. Have any of you volunteers ever been along the lake shore?"

"A couple of times," Fairchild said promptly. He slid a finger under his hatband and scratched his head. "You might have something, Colonel.

There's peninsulas run into the lake all along this end. Some're flat, some rocky, and there's one just ahead of us that's pure rock. Might turn into a meat grinder if we stormed it. But if we could get around it and on the Injuns' back, we could sure raise hell."

"What's our chances of getting past the point?"

"Depends on how many warriors they've got there. Which might not be many, since they seem to have got used to the notion that you're tryin' to join Bernard south of 'em."

Green nodded. "There's no way to set it up with Bernard, but if we broke through on the north we might have fairly easy going along the edge of the lake and could connect with his north flank without his help. All it requires is to take that point and hold it long enough for the command to pass around it. What do you others think?"

"Looks like our only chance," Mason said grumpily. "But I wish we could use cannon."

"I've wished that all day. How about the rest of you?"

Jackson, Perry and Adams nodded their approval. Night was not far off, and they would all feel better if they had contact with Bernard by then.

CHAPTER V

Fairchild was the only volunteer captain with a personal knowledge of the terrain they were about to make a bid for, and he was assigned to lead off. He swung his frontiersmen to the end of the line, the two regular companies also assigned to the spearhead moving in behind him. Green ordered a stepped-up fire pattern on the southern sector, hoping to convince the Indians that another assault on the bloody ridge was coming. Under this cover, Fairchild's men moved close enough to the point of rocks to make out its fog-skirted base. They were considerably cheered when they drew no fire from it.

"Mebbe it's gonna work," Yost whispered to Zack. "First time all day we've caught 'em napping."

"If we have," Zack agreed.

"Quiet, there," a corporal muttered.

Yost swore at him under his breath, and Zack looked back at the rocky point, around which they had to swing when Fairchild gave the order. It seemed a hellish while since they had rolled out of their blankets in the darkness of dawn to live the weirdest, wildest, most heartbreaking day of their lives. Somehow Zack had escaped the Modoc bullets, which had felled so many of them, but his hands were gashed and bleeding from rock cuts; his knees, hips and elbows were abraded and sore; and the razorlike edges of the rocks had ruined a good pair of boots.

Word to move forward came man to man down the line, which began to file toward the lake end of the point. The fog was no thinner there or over the lake than on the lavas. They reached the point and passed around it without difficulty, a rocky overhang extending above their heads and concealing them from possible sharpshooters higher up. On the far side of the point they found a recess in the rock, its floor a mixture of cinders and coarse sand. There was another point beyond but easier to pass than the first one. The sneak out-flanking maneuver began to look more than possible, and Fairchild moved his company across the recess, halted it and sent word back to Perry and Mason to come on. Once the three lead companies were lodged here, the other four could pass behind them and go on east toward Bernard.

But from above them came a crash of rifles.

The volunteers flung themselves flat on the coarse grits, but two men fell in heedless, all-gone spills. Zack saw in dismay that one of them was Bill Minto, the other Yost, cut down on either side of him. A second volley came from the Modocs on the low rim to the south, barely visible in the fog, and pinned him down. Somehow the Indians had caught on to the movement, but it must have surprised them. The warriors up there were shrieking for help from their flanks and rear even while they sent a rain of death into the recess below them.

"Back, boys!" Fairchild shouted. "Get under that overhang!"

There was nothing to do but make a bold run for cover, and the volunteers scrambled for the position indicated. The man beyond Minto called that he was dead, but Yost, when Zack crawled to him, still breathed. With bullets peppering the ground around him, he somehow managed to drag the wounded man into cover and join the new line that had started to return fire.

Instead of discouraging Perry's company, the eruption of gunfire, beyond the point from it at first, caused it to hurry forward to help. It came around the point into another Modoc volley, in which Perry and a lieutenant, Kyle, who were in the lead, went down. But the rest of the company boiled on, and Zack saw Del for the first time all day. He had taken charge of the lead platoon. These men took position on the west side of the recess, across the open from the volunteers. On their heels came the rest of the company, followed by Mason's unit.

The reinforcements whacked a hot fire at the rim above, and for a while it looked as if they could immobilize it enough for the plan to go forward without a loss that would be ghastly. But with surprising speed Modoc reinforcements came from somewhere to whip up the hottest fire-fight so far in the day's ill-fated operations. Fairchild's company, cut off from the regulars by the open space, was in a perilous position that would be fatal if the regulars were driven out. The Modocs knew that and seemed to be marshaling even more sharpshooters.

Zack bent over Yost, who was hit hard, the bullet having shattered his left hip. The first he knew the man was conscious was when Yost muttered, "Long walk gettin' here. Hell of a long walk back."

"You'll make it," Zack assured him.

"Bill Minto O.K.?"

"No, Ernie. He's dead."

Over in Del's company Perry, although hit badly in the shoulder, had resumed command. Kyle, who had taken a bullet through the arm, was also back in the fight. But it had grown impossible for more reinforcements to move in from the main command. There was no room for them to take position, and if they tried to pass behind the line and go on along the shore, they would be cut to pieces on the open ground they would have to cross. Every Modoc in the lavas seemed to be a crack shot, and they were in no mood to be driven off the rim. Perry sent a report on the situation to Colonel Green, the courier having to move back around the point under the overhang.

John Fairchild had reached a conclusion similar to Perry's. "All we can do is hang and rattle till night," he told his uneasy men. "Then

59

mebbe we can use the dark to link up with Bernard."

"Or get outta here," somebody muttered.

The looks he got from those who heard him indicated that they all preferred to quit the lava beds completely.

Night was close at hand. And less than an hour before it came the fog ironically lifted for just a few minutes, then socked in again. At the main command post on the bluff, Colonel Wheaton concluded that any further pressing of the hapless attack was useless. Twice the number of men at his disposal would be required to storm the Indians in that natural fortress with any hope of success. During the lift in the fog he signaled Bernard to withdraw the eastern force to a position he could hold for the night and to return to his outpost east of the beds the next day. He sent a cease-fire down to Colonel Green and, shortly afterward, the order to retreat from the lavas.

At the point of rocks, by then, there were three dead and half a dozen wounded. But there was no chance to move until full night could cloak them from the humiliatingly small force of Modoc warriors opposed to them. Meanwhile the line elsewhere began to pull back from the slag hell that, as much as the Indians, had defeated it, expecting at every step the added embarrassment of a counterattack by the Modocs. Able-bodied men helped, carried or dragged along as many of the wounded as they could reach, and more were hit trying to help those who had fallen in positions exposed to the Indians.

Drunk on their accomplishment, the Modocs split the dusk-sooted fog with shrieks and whoops and stayed on the command's heels, peppering it, now and then picking off a straggler. But slowly, painfully and until well in the night the command came out of the lavas, boots worn out and worse, feet and hands bleeding, clothing frayed and stained with blood. For ten hours it had fought savagely and in complete futility against a foe most of the men had not even seen.

Among the last to reach the encampment of the bluff top were Perry's and Mason's regulars and the California volunteers. Shortly after nightfall this detachment had crept out of its cul-de-sac, bringing its dead and wounded. By the time it reached the army camp the fog had begun to move, clearing off the lavas and settling on the far, north shore of Tule Lake. Out in the lavas fires sprang up on the sharp peaks. In their shadowy light danced the Indians, within sight but out of range of the troops. They were celebrating the victory brought to them by the vast mystic powers of Curly Doctor.

The pickets around the army bivouac were doubled that night, while the command slept the sleep of total exhaustion. But there was light at the command post and at the hospital tent, where the surgeon and his orderlies worked with the wounded. Only nine of the gravely hurt had been brought in, while there had been thirty-two walking cases. Still in the lavas, somewhere, were an unreckoned number of men unaccounted for.

The next morning the Modocs were out on the battlefield in the first light, the fog now vanished, picking up soldiers' guns and cartridge belts, stripping bodies, finishing off the wounded not recovered by the troops by crushing their heads with rocks. By the time military patrols reached the scene, there was nothing left to recover but a staggering number of bodies, naked and mutilated. These were buried at the base of the bluff, along with the dead brought in during the retreat and four of the wounded who had died at the hospital. Thirty-nine in all, soldiers and citizen-soldiers, over whom taps rolled for the last time.

The Modocs came to the edge of the lava beds and hootingly invited the "Boston" soldiers to come back for a return engagement. Instead of accepting, Wheaton ordered the sullen command to return to its base at Van Bremer's ranch, a dozen miles to the west.

A lot had happened in the two-and-a-half-day stay at the lavas. Defeat was galling enough, but pride was the lesser part of the problem. Wheaton saw the need for additional troops, which would have to be brought in from posts more distant than those occupied by the 1st Cavalry. That posed a proportionate problem in logistics, and the officers and men saw what had promised to be little more than a patrol in force shape up as a long campaign.

Especially did Zack Buckman see an extensive delay in his return to the Wagonwheel: Del and he had come through unscratched, for which he was grateful, but the outcome of the battle was a bitter disappointment. Bill Minto was dead, fated to sleep forever there at the edge of the bluff, leaving his crippled brother Johnny alone on Wildhorse Creek, next door to the Sleeper clan. Ernie Yost, before he left for the army hospital at Fort Klamath, expressed his own concern. It was more for the man he had ridden for than for himself.

"Johnny Minto's on his lonesome. If you're right about the Sleepers, and they knock him off his spread, Hollis Brown'll come next. And Hollis ain't so young any more. With you tied up here God knows how long and me in the hospital mebbe to lose a leg — well, count 'em, Zack. The able-bodied men down there to stand against them four sons of bitches."

Zack shook his head glumly. There was Fred Trinkler and Ridge Agee, since Martin Dunes was too unpredictable to count on either side of an internal fight in the Wagonwheel. "Forget it, Ernie, and get yourself in shape to fork a horse again," he said.

Ambulances, some of them only wagons, hurried down from Linkville, got away with the wounded. Then camp was broken and the weary command marched back over the ridges and plateaus to the big stock ranch on Willow Creek.

At the next morning's roll call there wasn't a company that didn't have men fail to answer. Deserters. Men who wanted no more of the Modocs and the lava beds.

Quarrels broke out among the officers over the conduct of the battle. A newspaper reporter hurried up from San Francisco to write a deriding story of the four hundred soldiers who had failed to dislodge a mere handful of Indians. The account, which was sent east over the telegraph, was especially critical of Wheaton. The brevet general, in turn, fired off a letter to the Columbia Department at Fort Vancouver, demanding an artillery company with mortars and at least three hundred infantry troops before he would take another command into the lavas.

From Van Bremer's it was only a ten-mile ride over the plateau to the Sleeper spread at the foot of the Wildhorse Hills. Zack was not surprised when, a few days after the command's return, Purdy rode in with Rip, one of his hellion sons. Whatever brought them, they stopped at Fairchild's camp, and both men wore a look of sullen hostility.

Fairchild happened to be on hand, and, without a greeting, Purdy stared at him with his small, hard eyes and said, "What kind of pull've you got with the army, John, to get it planted here, where it protects you and Van Bremer and Dorris? Where do the rest of us look for protection?"

Fairchild's face was already the color of an old

saddle, but Zack and the others standing near saw it darken considerably. His own ranch lay only a few miles to the northwest, on the Cottonwood. The base was here, instead of in the wastes where the bivouac had been, because Van Bremer's was on one of the two roads connecting the Nevada railroad with the Shasta country and southern Oregon and it afforded plenty of good water and fresh beef for the mess.

"I got no influence with the army, Sleeper," Fairchild said in a curiously softened voice. "If you don't like the way it's runnin' things, why don't you ride on over to headquarters and take it up with the general? He'd be mighty happy to have your advice."

Purdy turned his head and spat out a brown squirt of tobacco juice. "He could use it. If I couldn't salt down them Modocs with the help he had, I'd sure make an effort to keep 'em corralled in them rocks. Be damned if I'd be off here a dozen miles away, lettin' 'em whack in and out as they please."

Aversion filed its way along Zack's long spine, a feeling that the Sleepers were here for something besides making nuisances of themselves. "Seen any Modocs rammin' around, Purdy?" he said.

Sleeper eyed him. "Rip sure as hell did. A whole passel. Yesterday, at Martin Dunes' shack in Forbidden Canyon."

"Dunes? Either you're off your rocker, Purdy, or Rip is."

"Guess I know what I seen," Rip retorted. "I'd been over toward Black Ledge lookin' for strays and come back over the Coyotes. Took a look in the canyon from the rim when I come past. Always figured it was a good idea to keep an eye on that squaw man. And there they was, a good dozen."

"Modocs?"

"The same as shot the butts off'n you hombres."

Purdy relieved himself of another load of brown spittle. "Hooker Jim was one of 'em, and Dunes got his woman from Hooker's band when it used to camp in the Wagonwheel."

"That's probably why Hooker was there. They're old friends."

"Then how come," Sleeper drawled, "Rip and Frank found Johnny Minto shot and scalped this morning?"

"What's that?" Zack gasped.

Mention of the Minto name had alerted everyone in hearing distance. They had all known Bill, and he had been one of their number who had not come out of the lavas alive. Fairchild's countenance had taken on a rocky shock. He had known Johnny also, knew he had been a cripple, and that there had been bad blood between the Mintos and the Sleepers.

Purdy watched them with eyes that hinted of a savage enjoyment. "That's right. We figured Johnny ought to be warned there was Modocs lurkin' around the Wagonwheel. And there he was, dead in his own dooryard. With his hair lifted."

Zack didn't believe for a minute that that was what had really happened, but all he could do was stare at the wily, hard face that watched them so carefully.

Then Sleeper added, "Come on, Rip. Let's go see that sheepheaded gen'ril."

The pair rode on toward the bluecoat camp. Fairchild looked after them with questioning eyes. Zack had a powerful feeling that everything they had said before disclosing Johnny's murder had been calculated carefully. The outraged protest at the military force's being off here, with the whole west and south sides of the lavas left unguarded and the renegades free to leave the beds and range the country. The suspicion cast at Martin Dunes, the white man who turned against his people and took a woman from the band of Hooker Jim, who had already blazed a bloody trail through the basin.

More than one white man had removed someone who stood in his way and fixed it so it would be laid to the Indians. Word of Bill's death must have reached the Sleepers. And now the Minto range was vacant, to be taken and held by the next to claim it.

CHAPTER VI

Monk was holding the little tag of cattle his father and brothers were rebranding. Being up in the saddle, and east of the others, he was the first to see the two riders coming toward them from the south side of Hub Lake. Smelling trouble, he grinned and yelled at the men bent over a pig-tied steer at a sagebrush fire in the saucer bottom below him.

"Hey! We're gonna have company!"

Purdy straightened, a hot running iron in one hand and the other hand flattened on the back of his hip. His bearded face cracked into a drop-mouthed stare in the direction Monk pointed. Frank, who was helping Purdy at the fire, said something, but Purdy only muttered and went back to work. Beyond them, Rip, also mounted, was waiting to rope another steer for a turn under the iron. Rip looked off in the direction Monk indicated, scowled and scrubbed his sleeve across his mouth. They were mighty cool, seeing that they were putting the Big S on Minto cattle.

Monk sat in the raw cold of the January day, watching for another moment, then yelled again. "It's Trinkler and old Brown. We better get set for trouble."

Even then the men at the fire paid no attention.

The oncomers rode at a trot, straight toward this spot on the South Wildhorse, in the heart of range next door to their own. It looked like they had kept a jumpy eye on it since the Minto brothers were killed, since they couldn't have seen smoke as far off as their own spreads. Now Monk liked the cool way Purdy went right on with his work. He wished he could manage that kind of insolent indifference. He tried it, but there was still grease in his belly, half hope and half fear that lead would start flying.

He could see the anger on the faces of the two men as they rode nearer. Hollis Brown was a bantam, while Trinkler was a big man whose heavy features looked glazed over with ice. The pair rode up to the group at the fire. Monk moved his horse along behind them, not wanting to miss anything. The two took a look at the long yearling that had been thrown and pigged at the fire. Thy didn't seem at all surprised.

Old Hollis stared at Purdy with his mouth curled outward like the lip of a jug. "How do you expect to get away with that, Sleeper?" he demanded. "You know you've got no right to vent the Minto brand on them steers and slap on yours. Or are you gonna forge a bill of sale?"

Purdy didn't rile at that or even answer until Frank had untied the steer. It got up and ambled off, wearing a brand-new Big S over a vented M. Purdy nestled the iron in the coals again and finally looked at the visitors.

"Who needs a bill of sale for mavericks?" he

returned. "That's what this stuff is. Any claimers come along, they can argue ownership. It ain't your place to, Hollis."

Trinkler blazed. "I suppose you're takin' over the Minto boys' range the same flimsy way."

"It's vacant range," Purdy said, as if surprised that there would be any question about it. "Or it was till I started putting Big S steers on it. That makes it my range."

"Big S steers!" old Hollis snorted. "Which you're makin' right here with a runnin' iron!"

"I explained that," Purdy said patiently. "There's no need for you to get so exercised, Hollis. If any Minto kin show up, they can bring up the fine points of the case. Doubt any will. The Minto boys weren't married. Johnny told me once their kin's all back East."

Old Brown said with shaking bitterness, "You mangy on—" and bit it off real quick. Monk, listening closely, wanted to laugh.

"What were you about to say, Hollis?" Purdy said politely.

"Oh, hell, forget it. Come on, Fred."

They turned their horses and rode off. Only then did Purdy, after spitting a squirt of tobacco juice, permit himself to grin.

Built tall by his father's triumph, Monk said, "They see the handwritin' on the wall all right."

Purdy said sourly, "What do you mean by that?"

"They know who's next," Monk said triumphantly. They didn't figure him smart enough to see through all this.

"Damme," Purdy said to Frank. "That kid don't think of anything but orneriness."

"Sure he does," Frank remonstrated. "Sometimes he thinks about girls."

Rip said, "And thinkin' is about as far he's ever got."

"Like hell it is!" Monk began. They didn't know what all he did when they went down to the Comstock for a good time. He could tell them a few things, but he laughed awkwardly. They were only ribbing him because they felt good.

Brown and Trinkler hadn't liked what was happening to the Minto range and cattle, but they hadn't disputed that Johnny had been killed by Modocs. Monk didn't know any more about Johnny's dying, himself, than he had put together. Purdy and the older sons had been highly excited after word had reached them that Bill Minto had been killed in the big battle at the lava beds. The next day they had gone off somewhere, leaving Monk home to do chores. When they got back they had been talking about finding Johnny dead, scalped, and with his body stripped and mutilated. Then Purdy and Rip had ridden up to Van Bremer's ranch to report it to the army. When they got home again, Purdy had concentrated all their energy on cinching his claim to what the Mintos had left behind. Poor as he was at figuring, Monk reflected, he could add up that one.

He turned his head to see Brown and Trinkler disappearing in the blue-chilled distance. His father and brothers had returned to their work, forgetting him. He wondered what he would have to do to make them accept him as a grown man and their equal.

It took two more days to convert everything that had been the Mintos' to Sleeper property. By then Monk had discovered that the move against old Hollis Brown was not to follow immediately, as he had been sure it would. He was still sure it would come eventually, but all at once Purdy and the older boys started talking about the cattle and horses left ownerless, or at least unwatched, in the country east of Tule Lake, where Hooker Jim had killed off so many ranchers. Chance Colby had been one of the murdered cattlemen, and his C iron begged to be run on into a Big S. There would be slicks on the other deserted ranges too, for nobody had been able to work his cattle properly after the Indian pot began to boil. Zack Buckman was tied up with the California Rifles, away from Pistol Pass, which would be a good way to slip some of the Tule Lake stuff into the Wagonwheel and across to the Wildhorse Hills.

Monk was not surprised when, one morning after they finished with the Minto stock, he was told to stay home and take care of the chores. Purdy, Frank and Rip made up a pack and rode off toward Pistol Peak, saying that they would be back in a day or two. Monk resented being eliminated again and nursed his hurt feelings for nearly an hour before it came to him that it might be a break. For the first time he could remember, he had a couple of days of complete freedom.

What he would do with it was not decided for him until the next forenoon, while he was returning to headquarters after a look at some steers Purdy kept on the west range. Riding along the slope above the gap between the Wildhorse and Coyote hills, he saw riders below him on the trail from the east end of the Wagonwheel. Through travelers sometimes traveled by way of the Wagonwheel, but he recognized the cut of the trio even at some distance. Reining over into cover, he waited, letting them pass closer below him to make sure.

He had been right. They were Hollis Brown, Fred Trinkler and Ridge Agee, whose outfit was on the east end of Hub Lake. Except for Martin Dunes and himself, they were the entire male population of the Wagonwheel at present. They were either going up to the army headquarters or to Yreka. Either ride would take them the rest of the day.

Monk wondered briefly if they were going to tell the army people or the sheriff at Yreka about Purdy's brand venting and his grab of the Minto range. That could be troublesome, but he was unable to concentrate on the matter, for another thought had floated into his mind. Dora, Agee's pretty, red-headed daughter, would be alone at the ranch. Just the two of them in the whole Wagonwheel, since Dunes and his girl didn't count as white folks and neighbors. Monk felt a hot fullness in his face while he watched the riders out of sight, moving on toward the Van Bremer plateau. Once through the gap, he saw, they turned west. They were going to Yreka, and he didn't give a damn if it was to make law trouble for the Sleepers. They couldn't be back before nightfall, if they returned at all that day.

Monk rode home as fast as his horse would carry him, then told himself to whoa up, since he didn't want to rush the thing so fast he ruined it. After unsaddling, he rubbed down the horse, tossed it a fork of wild hay, then went into the house. He built a fire in the rusty iron stove and started a meal, and while he waited for it to cook he had a snort from the jug Purdy kept under his bunk. The fiery liquor scalded all the way down, but once settled it began to build confidence in his plan. He ate and then decided, unwontedly, to get rid of a few whiskers before he started out.

There was only one razor in the family, and he had to hunt it up. It was dull, but he wasn't practiced in stropping it, so he lathered up with soap and tried to shave himself the way it was. When he had wetted and combed his mane of hair, he was pleased with his appearance. He slapped his hat against a knee, which hardly improved its mottled look, and tried it with a rake to the right and then with a rake to the left, which he liked better. He was about to get into his heavy old coat when his eye fell on the nearly new sheepskin Rip saved for visits to town. He donned that instead of his own coat, viewed himself once more in the cracked mirror, then held up the tails of the coat while he buckled on the gun rig he had decided to wear, as much for effect as because of danger.

Ten minutes later he was riding east across the long basin floor. The air had grown colder, but there were hardly any clouds or other signs of an approaching storm. He decided to go down the south side of the lake, for he had never visited the actual headquarters of Brown and Trinkler, which would be deserted. He slanted off in that direction, letting the horse go along at a comfortable trot. Old Sentinel Peak rose off to his left, and farther left were the low lines of the Coyote Hills. And Forbidden Valley, he thought contemptuously. Pretty soon there wouldn't be a place in the Wagonwheel forbidden to the Sleepers.

Due to the flow of the spokelike creeks into the lake, the ranch buildings of the men who had settled around the lake were only a mile or so apart. He paid no attention to the Minto place, where he and his family had already made themselves at home. But when he reached old Brown's setup on the West Lizard, he stopped long enough to look around. It was nothing special — a cabin and outbuildings and a few corrals. No woman had ever lived there; Brown's only company had been Ernie Yost, who was in the army hospital at Fort Klamath. Monk rode on and passed Trinkler's place with hardly more than a cursory glance. Time enough to look it over after it became Sleeper property.

It was midafternoon when he found himself on the rim skirting one side of Moccasin Creek and its narrow valley, where he had more than once taken a secret look at Ridge Agee's house, hoping to catch a glimpse of Dora and sometimes succeeding. He didn't expect her to be outdoors in the dry winter cold, for down here there was a wind off Hub Lake. Noting only that smoke lifted from the outside chimney of a rock fireplace, he rode on down the slant to the valley floor.

He could not remember having lived on a place where a woman's influence was evident, like it was at Agee's, for the shreds of memory he retained of his mother were not associated with family and family life. But here it was plain to see a woman's influence. The windows were curtained. There was no clutter of tools and equipment, which made the other houses in the basin hardly different from the barns. He noticed these qualities as he rode calmly into the ranch yard. He had not hallooed the house in advance. He didn't want to be caught sneaking up, but he figured it wouldn't hurt his chances if he took Dora by surprise.

He succeeded in part, for he had ridden to the edge of the porch before the door opened a crack and he saw Dora peeking out at him.

"Howdy, Dora," Monk said amiably. "Was that your pa I seen ridin' out with them fellas, Yreka way?"

She stiffened and didn't answer him. The door crack narrowed when he swung out of the saddle. He knew she was ready to slam the door and bar it in his face if he didn't talk just right.

"Got a reason for asking," Monk resumed. "After I seen them fellas, I found a Modoc sign. Come down to warn Brown and Trinkler, but neither one was home. Come to me it could've been them and your pa I seen this morning, too far off to recognize."

He saw he had disarmed her enough as to his own intentions to listen to him. She let the door open a little wider. He could see pretty nearly all of her then, from the red hair she combed in a bun to the long legs that suggested themselves beneath her apron and skirt. She said skeptically, "What kind of sign did you find?"

"Enough to worry me," Monk said with a shake of the head. "You know Hooker Jim's old camp over at Kettle Springs? Well, some of 'em camped there last night. Near as I could tell, they went on into the Lizards instead of back to the lavas. They're keepin' their eye on us, you can bet. It sure scared me, because pa and the boys're gone."

She swallowed and said, "What'll we do? Pa and them won't be home till tomorrow sometime. There's just —" She broke off.

"Just us," he agreed. "But they got me to deal with, Dora, before they'll ever lay hands on you. Mind if I come in to the fire? That lake wind's sure cold."

"I —"

She didn't like that idea either, but he had frightened her to a point where a Sleeper looked better than a Modoc with a scalping knife. She stepped back and let him come in. He noticed how her hands trembled when she closed the door. He walked on to the fireplace and put his back to it. The warmth felt good after his long ride. She remained by the door, and in the corner beyond her a rifle stood against the wall. He knew it was loaded.

He said solicitously, "Your pa oughtn't to have kept you out here after the Injun trouble started."

"He wanted to send me to Yreka, but I wouldn't go."

She looked like she wished mightily that she had. He watched her, surprised at how pretty she was close up, impressed by the control she kept of herself in spite of the fictitious danger he had painted. Her waiting within reach of the rifle showed that she wasn't exactly easy about him either. He hadn't expected to care whether she thought well or ill of him, once he got in here with her. But he did care. He wished she felt enough of the wild excitement booming through him to be glad he was here, and not just to protect her from Indians.

She said uneasily, "Where'd your folks go?"

"Oh, off somewhere," he said vaguely. "They're always rammin' around." He knew at once that he had said the wrong thing. The fact that the Sleepers were always on the prowl was one of the main objections their neighbors had to them. Or it had been the big one until Johnny Minto got killed, giving them something more definite to worry about. He looked at her in sudden intentness. "What packed your pa and them off to Yreka?"

"I — don't know."

The way she looked away convinced him that she did know, and her refusal to say meant it was something she couldn't say to him. So it was about Johnny Minto and the Minto range and livestock. Monk shifted his weight uneasily under her cool eyes, growing angry from her distrust, whipping the anger into disdain of whether she liked or hated him.

She thought she was smart, staying close to that gun, but maybe he was a little smarter. He cocked his head in sudden intentness, listening and watching the darkening of her face. Then he crossed to the door and opened it, looking out carefully. She had moved toward the rifle, getting out of his way.

Reaching a hand, he said quietly, "Loan me that rifle. There's somebody in the brush down by the lake."

"Oh no."

"Quick."

He kept his eyes on the lake growth but heard her moving. Then he felt the rifle against his reaching hand. He grasped it, laughed and stepped back into the room, kicking the door shut.

Dora gasped. "The whole thing was a rotten, dirty trick!"

He tried to master Purdy's silky mockery. "It was? Now ain't that a pity. Not even Modocs around. Just you and me."

"Monk Sleeper," she blazed, "you get off this place!"

It was better to have her act like he was dirt, for that way he felt no responsibility to her at all. The readiness came into him, the disdain of what happened to her as long as he had his way. He unloaded the rifle and dropped the shells into the pocket of his sheepskin, then stood the gun at the side of the fireplace. He let his eyes rake over her.

"No use bein' so hoity-toity," he told her. "Before mornin' comes, we're gonna have us a time. You'll like it too good to make me trouble afterward. You'll want to marry up with me."

"You conceited, unspeakable beast!"

He laughed and went for her. Her body, when he caught hold of her, was soft and warm — and much stronger than he had expected. She jerked loose, ducked and went under his arm, instead of running away as he expected. By the time he hauled around, she had caught up the rifle, holding it by the barrel. He saw the stock end coming at him, could almost hear it swoosh, and threw up an arm. The thud and pain reached his brain together. With a curse he clapped his free hand to a tingling, pain-shooting elbow. He bent, gusting air when the rifle butt rammed into his belly.

"So it's true what they say!" Dora panted. "You've got the body of a bull and the brain of a louse!"

He could only gape at her, gagging for breath. His tingling elbow had him crazy, and he hadn't known how bad it hurt to get hit in the belly like that. She had the rifle stock swung back, ready to give it to him again. He tried to wave her away with his workable arm.

"Don't —"

"Give me those shells from your pocket or you get it across your thick head."

The cartridges were on his workable side. He obeyed and watched her load the rifle again. Then she backed off, the barrel pointing right at his heart. She looked ten feet tall while she stood watching him, catching her breath.

She had her wind back, and she did some thinking before she spoke again. "My father would kill you if I told him about this. Maybe that's what you Sleepers want — to get him to come gunning so you can gang up and murder him. So I'm not going to tell him this once. But if you give me cause again, I'll tell every man in the Wagonwheel. They'll string up your whole rotten family. Now get riding before I decide to rid the world of one of you right now!"

There wasn't a trace left of the randy drive that had brought him here. Monk turned and, still unable to stand erect, lurched to the door and across the porch. She was standing in the doorway when, finally, he had hoisted himself into the saddle. The bore of the rifle looked big as a tin cup.

He rode due north until he cut the basin road, which ran from the Moccasin to the coyote gap. By then the blows Dora had given him had stopped hurting. His brain had thawed out, letting him see the extent of his defeat at the hands of a slip of a girl. His life wouldn't be worth living if Rip knew about that, which was the only reason Monk saw to be glad Dora had decided to keep it to herself. If he had got what he had come down here after, he would have boasted rather than tried to keep it quiet. And his father and brothers would have promoted him, finally, to the status of a real grown man.

He had gone only a few miles toward home when he grew aware of a rider coming toward him on the trail. He scowled, remembering that the only other white man in the basin, at the moment, was Martin Dunes. He didn't relish meeting Dunes face to face, but he had been humbled plenty for one day and rode stubbornly on down the trail. In a few moments he realized that the oncomer was Zack Buckman.

Puzzled, Monk rode on toward him, a rasping uneasiness in his shoulders that Zack always induced. Zack would have passed on with no more than a stiff nod, but Monk reined in.

"What're you doin' here?" Monk said with a loose grin. "Thought you were signed up with the Rifles for the duration of the war."

Zack stopped his horse and regarded him with eyes cold as the wintry day. He pondered a moment, then said, "Guess it'd be a good idea to send your old man word at that. Tell him I'm back to stay awhile, Monk."

Monk gaped. "How come?"

Zack's thin grin suggested that he knew his return would be anything but welcome news to Purdy. Instead of explaining, he rode on.

Monk continued his ride westward, lost in thought. Zack had sounded like he knew Purdy counted on the war's keeping him away from the Wagonwheel a long time yet. His puzzling return would bring complications — one immediately. Purdy and the boys aimed to bring stolen cattle into the Wagonwheel by way of Pistol Peak, figuring Zack wasn't there. Monk knew he had ought to warn them, but they had given him no idea of where they might be found short of a lot of hunting in country badly menaced by the Modocs. Let them find out for themselves, he thought. Then the next time they might let him in on things.

CHAPTER VII

A frown deepened on Zack's face while he rode in to the Agee house, for there was an unnatural stillness to the place, a look of complete desertion even though smoke rose from the chimney into the chill wind from the lake. He had called out, which ordinarily would have brought somebody to a window or the door, but no one had appeared when he stopped at the steps and swung down. Then suddenly the door burst open and Dora stood staring at him, her expression of disbelief giving way to intense relief.

"Why, Zack — it's you!"

He was about to make a light retort when he realized that she was tense and pale. Crossing the porch swiftly, he said, "What's the matter, Dora? You had trouble?" His mind had gone to Monk, the first time he had wondered what the vicious kid had been doing in this end of the Wagonwheel.

"Oh no." She smiled with effort. "Pa went to Yreka, and, with Indians around, I guess I'm jumpy."

An Indian wouldn't have hailed the house, and she knew it. He said sternly, "Monk Sleeper been around here?"

"Why — what makes you ask?"

"Run into him up the trail. He give you trouble?"

"No." She smiled and added quickly, "What're you doing here? But come in first. You must be cold if you came down from Van Bremer's."

"I did and I am."

He followed her indoors, explaining that the war had bogged to a standstill. At the cost of much unmerited criticism from his superiors, the citizenry and the public press, Colonel Wheaton had insisted on heavy reinforcements before he would send men into the lava beds again.

"And he's dead right," Zack said somberly. "With their setup, one Modoc's the equal of twenty men trying to storm their stronghold. It'd be a crime to go back in on the same terms as the first time. But Wheaton convinced the high straps finally. He's getting the troops he wants."

It would take a month or more, however, for the reinforcements to arrive. Knowing the volunteers had better things to do than soldiering around camp, Wheaton had sent the California Rifles home until he had further need of them. The Oregon companies had moved north to guard the settlements on the Oregon side of the line.

"And Del's all right?" Dora said.

"Not even scratched in the fracas. He sent his love."

Zack wished his brother could have seen the way she closed her eyes for a moment. Nothing

85

she had ever said to Del could have told him so much. She said now, her ease and cheerfulness restored, "What am I standing here for? You must be starved."

"I sure am."

Zack had removed his coat, and he stood smoking his pipe by the fire while Dora hurried into the kitchen. He was still of the opinion that Monk Sleeper had been here, which had made her so boogery when he first arrived. But she showed no physical damage, and he knew her well enough to realize Monk could not have laid a hand on her without a fight that would have left marks on her. So he would respect her wishes and not press the matter.

Dora was back in a moment with a steaming cup of coffee. "I had a kitchen fire going." Handing him the cup, she added gravely, "You hear about Johnny Minto and how the Sleepers claim they found his body?"

He nodded. "Purdy and Rip come up to report it to the army."

"I bet they didn't report how they aimed to take over the Minto range and put their brand on the cattle and horses."

"I figured they'd grab the range," Zack said, scowling. "They take the livestock, too?"

"They sure did. Called the range vacant and the stuff on it mavericks." She told him about how Brown and Trinkler had found the Sleepers venting the M brand and about Purdy's cynical pretense. "That's what they went to Yreka

86

about. There's no proving who murdered Johnny, but that other business sure shows the Sleepers had a motive. Pa thought it would persuade the sheriff to investigate. Hollis and Fred witnessed it, but they wanted Pa along to do the talking."

"Good move," Zack said. "Because I think we're all on the list that Johnny headed."

She winced, then said in resignation, "No use shutting our eyes to it. Oh, Zack, I'm so glad you're back."

"Only for a while," he warned. "When they're set to try and crack that nut up there again, I'll have to go back."

He had supper with Dora and offered to stay overnight, but she insisted that she would be all right. So, in the last light of the day, he rode home to Pistol Peak, seeing it for the first time in weeks.

His headquarters stood beside the creek that came down from the peak and moseyed off toward Hub Lake. They weren't very showy — only a cabin of pine poles hauled from the hills and a few sheds and corrals of the same material. Yet it gave him a pride of possession when he came onto his range to see his home, with his and Del's cattle sprinkled across the flat, wearing the Double B that was their brand. Ridge Agee had looked out for the stuff during his absence. Zack wasn't worried about it, but he would ride the whole range as soon as he could, simply for the contact and satisfaction.

The cabin was bitterly cold and had a shut-up smell, but he soon had it warm and comfortable. Sitting by the fire for a while before turning in, he lighted a fresh pipe and tried to forget that a more vicious enemy than the Modocs threatened the basin. Captain Jack was at least fighting to retain what he considered his own. Purdy Sleeper was out to increase his holdings by dispossessing men who had been his neighbors.

Zack spent the next morning checking up on his affairs and finding them to his satisfaction. Late that afternoon Ridge Agee rode in from the direction of his spread.

"Dora said she told you why we went to town," Ridge said worriedly. He was a heavy-boned, powerful man with a look of toughness unequaled by the two other lake ranchers. Dora had got her red hair from him. "Thought I better ride over and tell you it done no good at all."

"Didn't expect it to," Zack admitted. "A dozen Pinkerton detectives couldn't pin Johnny's murder on the Sleepers now. But what about the venting?"

"The sheriff said he couldn't do anything about that except on complaint of the owners of the brand Purdy vented. Which we ain't. So there she rests." Ridge looked at Zack in the anger of impotence. "So we try and catch 'em in the act of murderin' one of the rest of us. Damn their bloody minds and black hearts. Old Purdy knew we couldn't get any real help from the law."

"I've got an idea," Zack said, "that he figured what to do in case the law did move in. When he come up to Van Bremer's he went out of his way to make it look like Martin Dunes is encouraging the Modocs to raid in the Wagonwheel. Everybody knows Dunes isn't happy about the rest of us being here. Rip claimed he'd seen a whole bunch of Indians in Forbidden Canyon right at the time Johnny was killed. Nothin' but a red herring."

"Could've been Indians, though," Ridge said. "Dunes hates us as bad as old Jack does."

"Dunes has no truck with us," Zack returned. "That don't prove he hates us."

"I know. Guess I'd rather think it was Modoc work. I'd sooner get killed by an arrow than a rattlesnake bite."

"I'm convinced we're in more danger from the rattlers, Ridge."

"Guess I am, too."

Ridge left, wanting to get back to Dora before dark. Zack spent the evening trying to figure a way to deal with the Sleepers but found nothing the rest of them could do but wait for developments. One thing he should do at once, however, was to warn Dunes that, like it or not, he was being involved in something that could be dirtier than the Indian war.

He struck off toward the Coyote Hills the first thing after breakfast the next morning. He had on occasion met up with the recluse and had discovered that, while not warming to him,

Dunes regarded him in a somewhat less hostile light than he did the other stockmen who had moved into the Wagonwheel.

The hidden canyon that Dunes had made a stronghold of his own was cut off from the Wagonwheel by a gorge which squeezed Coyote Creek between towering rock walls. The trail ran beside the creek, sometimes only a narrow shelf, and in case of need Dunes could hold it against a large force. Zack rode unhesitantly into the deep shadows and had met neither obstruction nor challenge when he emerged into the finger valley between the outlying and the major hills.

The cabin where Dunes had lived with his white daughter and a Modoc wife until the wife died a couple of years ago was at the upper end of the canyon, under the first higher hills. Zack called out to it as he approached, and when he rode up, Wendy was waiting in the dooryard, her hands gripped on a rifle.

She said, "Oh, it's you," and let the rifle trail.

He had seen her close up only a time or so, but she had remembered him. He said with a smile, "Howdy, Wendy. I've got to see your father. He home?"

"He — went hunting."

Her hesitation led Zack to suspect that she had not given him the truth. Possibly Dunes *was* working with the Modocs. He would not regard helping them to survive as a traitorous act. But Zack still couldn't see him helping in the way the Sleepers had hinted.

Wendy regarded him solemnly, with a child's open interest, and it struck him that she was a very pretty girl. He said, "There's something I figured he should know. You can tell him for me. Rip Sleeper says he saw a bunch of Modocs here in the canyon right at the time Johnny Minto was killed."

"That's a lie," she said promptly. "There haven't been any Modocs here since the war started."

"That's how I figured, but you tell Martin. He'll see what they're tryin' to do to him."

Wendy nodded her dark head. Zack was about to swing around and leave, but something in her eyes checked and held him there. Her lips formed what was almost a friendly smile. She didn't want him to go yet. That ghost of an expression showed him more clearly than anything she could have done the terrible loneliness of her life here, with a misanthrope whose views she might or night not share. He let the reins hang loose again and grinned at her.

"How've you been, Wendy?"

"I'm always fine." Her changing expression was also spectral, but he thought it was gratitude that he hadn't yet reconsigned her to solitude. Politely, she added, "And you?"

"The same."

She was about Dora's age, but as far as he knew the two girls had never got acquainted, which was a pity for both of them in this country of rough men and raw nature. She was a splendid specimen of womanhood, even in buckskin, with her dark hair loose and tumbling on her shoulders. Looking at her gave him a feeling he had experienced often when, from some observation point, he had looked out over a scene of clean, unspoiled natural beauty. Which was what she was — an unadulterated child of nature; and that was the way Dunes had wanted her to be.

Wanting to know more about her, he said, "You ever go hunting with Martin?"

"Quite a lot," she said.

"He ever taken you to Yreka or to one of the other towns?"

Her eyes brightened, but she shook her head.

"Would you like to see 'em?"

"I — reckon I would," she admitted.

Zack resolved that the next time he was within reach of a store he would buy her a present, a real feminine bauble, and her father's attitude about it be hanged. He was going to come here more often. He said, "Well, tell him what I said and that I'll be back in a few days. The Sleepers are out to make trouble that involves him as well as us. We ought to get together on it, no matter how he feels about the rest of us."

"He don't hate anybody," she said. "Except them."

"The Sleepers? Why them, if not the rest of us?"

"They killed my mother," she said in a flattened voice. "That's why they lied about Modocs being here. Purdy Sleeper's scared to death of Pa. If he could find a way to get rid of us, he'd do it."

"Where did this happen, Wendy?" Zack asked.

"Carson River. I don't remember. Pa only told me about it a while back. He caught Monk Sleeper on the rim, watching me. Pa said for me never to let him get near me and why they'd do us harm if they could." She moved the rifle. "That's why I got this when I heard you coming."

"You're not afraid of me, though?"

She shook her head. "I never was."

"Be all right for me to come back and see you?"

"I don't know." She looked at him gravely. "You could try and see."

"I sure will."

He rode back down Coyote Creek with a feeling of having discovered something he should have opened his eyes to long before. Wendy was not only a desirable girl in a country that contained few of any kind. She was also a girl badly in need of company, particularly that of her own race, especially that of a decent man her age. If he could be that to her, he was going to be, even if it meant taking on Martin Dunes.

It was late that night when something in the outer darkness interrupted Zack's sleep. He lay in a drowsy languor for a moment before he realized that he could hear the complaining rumble of cattle. After swinging out of the bunk, he crossed to the window on the side from which the sound came. Far out in the starshine he could see a massed shadow that moved slowly down the creek valley. Indians! And yet, if they had made a gather in the Wagonwheel, they were in the wrong place and going in the wrong direction.

He whirled, got hurriedly into his trousers, and pulled his boots onto bare feet. When he looked out the window again he saw that the cattle were being moved more swiftly. They were close enough then that he could make out a rider on this side and another in the rear, and he guessed the presence of a third on the far side. At the distance he couldn't begin to guess their race. After catching up his rifle, he rushed, half-clad, into the chilly outdoors.

Whoever they were, they were ignoring the nearness of his buildings, which was puzzling. He wondered if it was a legitimate herd being moved through the country from somewhere east. The drovers could be using the Wagonwheel and trailing at night in hopes of slipping unmolested around the Modocs in the lava beds. He estimated the herd at around a hundred head. There was a way to learn more about it.

He lifted the rifle to his shoulder and sent a shot ripping across the darkness, over their heads. The visible riders swung their horses toward him, stopping. Cupping his hands to his mouth, he yelled, "Hallo, out there! Who are you? Come over here and declare yourselves!"

He was only partly surprised when the two he

94

could see went like scared rats around behind the herd, vanishing on the far side. He fired another shot to let them know that he meant business. The shooting had lifted the cattle to a trot. He waited, puzzling. Legitimate drovers would have identified themselves speedily. Indians or vagrant rustlers would have made a fight for the loot they had gathered, wherever the steers came from. These people seemed mostly concerned with hiding themselves and their identity. It meant he would know them, and all at once he did.

He raced to the corral, roped a horse, made the rope into a hackamore, and went up bareback. The cattle were still trotting westward across the Wagonwheel. He went streaking out toward them, oblivious of the odds and the cold wind on his half-clad body. Cutting a circle that brought him around the rear of the herd, he saw three horsemen riding at a headlong gait toward the Coyote Hills.

That didn't fool him. They weren't Martin Dunes and a couple of renegade Indians gathering cattle to hide in the hills for Captain Jack to pick up. That was only what he was supposed to think. They were men who had been surprised and disconcerted to discover that he was home at Pistol Peak.

CHAPTER VIII

Zack pointed a finger. "See that brindle steer over there, Ridge?" Daylight was two hours old, and he had ridden over to get Agee as soon as the dawn had shown him what the night riders had unwillingly left on his range. "Recognize the brand?"

"Why, that's Chance Colby's C," Ridge said promptly.

"It sure is, and dead easy to blot into a Big S." They sat their horses at the edge of the little foreign herd, which had scattered along the creek. About half of it had turned out to be calves born since the last branding season but weaned away from their mothers. The mature stuff was all branded the same as the brindle. "I'd have been stumped as to where they came from," Zack continued, "if Purdy had been contented with what slick-ears he could pick up. The possibilities he seen in the Colby brand were too inviting, I guess."

Ridge nodded. He, too, was thinking of the sweeping ranges east of Tule Lake, vacated by Hooker Jim's massacre at the time of the outbreak. In many cases there was nobody left to claim the livestock now unattended and an open invitation to rustling. But Chance Colby had left a widow and three offspring, who had sought refuge in Linkville. The Sleepers were stealing what means of livelihood they had left.

"You sure must've thrown a shock into 'em last night," Ridge said. "And they won't be grateful to you for upsetting their game."

"They know where to find me," Zack said.

"What'll you do with 'em?" Ridge asked, nodding at the foreign cattle. "They're stolen. Maybe they'd persuade the sheriff, finally, that we've got more than Modocs on our hands."

Zack shook his head. "The Sleepers made sure I didn't see 'em close enough to swear it was them. The law'd say that if I can't swear it was somebody, it could've been anybody from anywhere after easy pickings in the raided country. But I wanted you to see the stuff and know how it got here, so I won't be stuck with stolen cattle on my range."

"You're hangin' onto 'em?"

"I'd like to see Sarah Colby get any benefit from 'em there is. So I'll put 'em on the other side of the peak, where they won't mix with Del's and my stuff, till I can see her and find out what she wants."

Ridge nodded his agreement. "Want me to help move 'em?"

"I can handle it."

Ridge left for home again. Zack spent the rest of the morning drifting the foreigners out of range of his own cattle, then turned his attention to his regular work.

He was surprised, that evening at dusk, when

Martin Dunes rode into the yard, forking an Indian pony. He carried a rifle in the manner of a man in country unremittingly hostile, and his face was locked tight. Yet he stepped down from the horse at Zack's invitation and came into the house, leaving the rifle leaning against the outside wall. There was no telling whether he felt easy, ill at ease or anything at all. He looked around the interior of the cabin without interest and shook his head impatiently at Zack's offer of a chair.

"You told the young'un you'd be back to see me," he said without preamble. He had a deep voice to go with his powerful chest. "Figured I'd save you the ride. You don't need to worry about me and Purdy Sleeper. I can take care of me and Wendy."

"I never doubted it," Zack returned. "Only wanted to warn you. Catching a man who's not looking's the way Purdy likes to do business."

"I ought to know that."

"So Wendy told me."

Dunes frowned. "I never thought to tell her to keep that to herself. Didn't expect her to be talking to anybody from the Wagonwheel."

"I've already forgot it, if that's what you want. But I'm curious to know why you didn't kill Purdy a long time ago."

Dunes glanced off at the stove. He had come here to discourage further visits to Forbidden Canyon, but he did not appear hostile beyond that. After a moment, he said, "Well, I had a

98

young'un I couldn't risk leavin' alone in the world. Not that I didn't figure I could kill him. But if I had, one of the others'd've got me. When I wasn't lookin', like you said."

"I know."

"It's the same reason I didn't kill him when he showed up in this country. But it's a little different now. Purdy Sleeper don't know just what day I'll figure she don't need me no more."

Zack looked the man straight in the eye when he said, "How'll she get over needing you, the way you keep her shut off from the world?"

"I've taught her to take care of herself."

"And be satisfied with what you've given her?"

"She's satisfied." Dunes was staring at him, still without notable resentment. He seemed to realize that the question came out of sympathy more than as censure. "She's got all she wants."

"She isn't satisfied, and she hasn't got all she wants," Zack returned. "She's the lonesomest, hungriest girl I ever seen."

"Lonesome? Hungry? What for?"

"For what you took away from her, the same as Purdy Sleeper took away her mother." Zack drew in a breath, watching his visitor. "Are you man enough to hear the truth, Dunes? She told me she don't remember what happened to her mother. She don't have your bitterness to comfort her, to keep her there in Forbidden Canyon. It's you keeps her there, not her own feelings."

"You don't know what you're talking about," Dunes muttered.

"I think I do. It wasn't her idea for you to come here so I won't have reason to go back there. It was yours, and you couldn't remove my reason. Which is Wendy, your daughter. Until she tells me to stay away and makes me believe she means it, I'm coming over there to see her."

Dunes shook his shaggy head, more in bewilderment than in negation.

"Am I a Monk Sleeper?" Zack said harshly. "Are you afraid of something like that?"

"No." Then, in abrupt and stubborn anger, Dunes said, "She don't want truck with white people. She was raised an Injun. When this trouble's over, she'll be with 'em again. If she wants a man, he'll be an Injun."

"Not if I can help it."

Dunes looked at him for a moment. He made no threats. When something he was putting through his mind was finished, he turned without a word and left.

Zack watched him ride off into the night that had come down on the Wagonwheel, strongly moved by Dunes' personal tragedy yet stubbornly bent on not letting it reflect on an innocent girl any longer. He pondered this with no clear understanding of the feeling that had grown in him for Wendy. Pity was too poor, too mean a word for it. One thing was sure. It was a powerful feeling. . . .

There was evidence, when Zack rode out of Pistol Gap on its far side a few mornings later, that another of the sometimes balmy Februaries known to the country was being born. The air was motionless, fragrant with the first hints of spring. From the pass he could see far into the eastern half of Tule basin, where Purdy Sleeper had done the rustling. Off to the left, sharp in the early light, lay the tortured sea of slag that had become hell's own battleground. He could see the vapors hanging above Tule Lake beyond. East from there was the land rise that blocked off Clear Lake, with which Tule was united by the long loop of Lost River.

On the near side of these landmarks lay the army outpost commanded by Captain Bernard, whose garrison, except for patrol duty, was marking time. This was Zack's destination, a ride of a couple of hours, and he struck down the slope in that direction, his pipe in his teeth, the danger from entering country regularly haunted by skulking Modocs receding under the serene influence of the morning.

Bernard was at the camp when Zack arrived in the late forenoon. Long seasoned on the frontier, the portly, weather-stained captain had no use for military starch, and he talked with Zack in person. He listened in growing anger to the report of cattle rustling in the vacated country, which was east and north of the camp. Zack did not name the men he suspected.

"We'll sure keep our eye on it," Bernard promised. "And if we catch rustlers in there, they'll be shot like any other looter in a war theater. I hate the sight of a carrion-picking buzzard."

"They always show up." Zack turned to leave, then swung back. "Captain, you got any idea when they'll call us volunteers back?"

Bernard shook his head and said with a sigh, "It gets farther off all the time. Colonel Wheaton's critics're making their weight felt. There's a rumor that he's to be replaced. And another almost as discouraging. They say Washington thinks it can negotiate a settlement with Jack. If they try, we'll sit here all summer while they learn what all the other negotiators learned. Then we'll still have Jack to root out of there with arms. A job, I can tell you, that I don't relish. But it's got to be done, and I'd like to get at it."

"I agree with you," Zack said. "All the way."

He headed back to the Wagonwheel with a feeling that he had done his best to protect the unguarded cattle that had drawn Purdy Sleeper's eye. But when it came to the range and cattle in the Wagonwheel itself, there was no such protection possible.

He was halfway home when he came upon cow signs in abundance that had not been there on his ride north. Reining in, he stared puzzledly at the hoof-scuffed, sandy earth, which had dried a lot under the warm sun. He looked at the fresh droppings, at the extent of the new trail that came from the south and — he saw when he swung his horse — slanted off to the northwest along the edge of the southern lavas. The sign had been made by a bunch as large as the one he had had on his hands the last few days. He whirled the horse again and stared into the south, toward Pistol Peak. The drive had come from that direction. He would have bet his life, suddenly, that it was the same herd.

With an angry pinch of the lips, he changed direction and rode at a canter along the easily followed trail of the cattle. They were being hurried, and he could pick out the tracks of a horse here and there. The tracks were shoeless, suggesting an Indian pony, but he wasn't swallowing that without more evidence. The trail led him northwest for a while, then veered north into the first scattered outliers of the lava beds.

That matched with the unshod horses, for the Modocs kept their beef cattle and spare horses in the grassy openings in the south end of the lava field, many of which held cisterns of rain water. He slowed but rode on, puzzling over whether it was real or a cunning deception. Another Indian indication was the unhesitant way the drive had kept on, straight toward a cleft in the first rock ridge ahead of him. The area on this side of the ridge was scabby and broken. An undefined uneasiness rose in him, but he slid his rifle out of its boot and, with a stubborn set of the jaw, rode on.

The sudden flicking of an ear of his horse was all that saved him. He had come even with a scabby, brush-fringed fumarole, still a little short of the gap that had swallowed the cattle. He reacted to the horse's sudden awareness of sound and reared back on the reins, bringing the animal to a sliding halt just as the crash of a rifle split the silence. The bullet meant for him hit the rearing horse instead. The scream of the creature echoed the shot, and Zack barely cleared himself before the animal sank down and rolled heavily onto its side. He squirmed around, protected by the horse's twitching body for the moment. More shots crashed in the desert quiet, and he saw the smudge of smoke over there by the fumarole. Judging the position of the man concealed by sagebrush and rock, he hammered in two shots as fast as he could send them.

There was no response. The wounded horse had stopped threshing, and again the rocky desert was awesomely quiet. For a while longer Zack held himself motionless, hoping that would tempt his assailant to investigate, on the assumption that he was hurt or dead. Finally he took off his hat and let the peak of the crown show slightly above the horse and grew puzzled when this drew no fire. Maybe it was a game of patience, he thought, with the ambusher waiting for his nerves to force him to make a better target of himself.

Then he began to wonder. This part of the lavas displayed the oddities that marked the rest. Suspicion squirmed in his mind as to how his attacker had got into place without leaving a getaway horse somewhere near. And, perhaps, having pumped in a hail of lead, had got away again, having no taste for shooting it out. Zack began to push himself back from the horse, changing position without sacrificing the dead animal's protection. Then, his rifle ready, he sprang up, his eyes glued to the fumarole.

There still was no response. Ducked over and weaving, he ran forward without drawing fire.

The formation was like a hole bubbled up in boiling mush, and that in essence was what it was, a hole created by escaping gas and heat in ages past, when the flow was molten. Some of the holes were connected to long tubes and underground caverns in which a man would walk. Peering in, he saw that was the case with this one. There was a passage, and the other end must be over there in the lava ridge or on its blind side. He had been expected, which meant he had been decoyed. Someone had fallen back through the subterranean passage to waylay and kill him.

There was more to be read. Zack stared at a dribble of dark blotches on the bottom of the hole, not immediately notable because of the red lava rock. The same dribble was on the projection by which the ambusher had climbed out to shoot. He had been hit, and that was what had caused his retreat, as much as a disinclination for a standoff gun fight. Zack swung a quick look toward the gap. There had been more than one man with the cattle. Whoever had tried for him, his companions were still able-bodied. Zack knew he was in no position to take on several of them singlehanded.

He hated to leave his saddle on the dead horse, but they could come out at any moment to see if they had had equal success in killing its rider. Turning, he began to make his way back along his own course, keeping cover between himself and the gap.

By the time he felt he could relax his hurried pace, bearing south, he was pretty clear on what had happened. The Sleepers had kept tabs on him ever since he had disrupted their drive with the stolen cattle. When, that morning, they had seen him ride north toward Bernard's outpost, they must have guessed his purpose.

It would have been Purdy's scheming mind which saw the chances to dissociate the Sleepers from the steers that so abruptly had become dangerous to them. At the same time they could lure Zack into an ambush, knowing he would be back along the same trail within a few hours. Had one of those shots achieved its purpose, Zack knew, someone would eventually have found his body looking the way Johnny Minto's had when found. That, with the cattle in the Modocs' holding area, would cover Purdy's snake tracks, blame Jack's band for it, and rid Purdy Sleeper of an enemy.

It had been a mighty close call.

In another hour he was back on his own range, hiking down from Pistol Pass toward his headquarters. The walk on riding heels had been tiring, and there was no longer need to hurry. Yet, as he drew in sight of his buildings, he found himself moving faster. There was a strange horse in his corral, and one that looked familiar. He was running by the time he got near enough to be sure it was the private horse that Del kept with him.

Del had seen him coming and left the house and was walking to meet him. His pleasure in the surprise he had given his brother was mixed with a puzzled concern.

"What in blazes put you afoot?" was his first remark.

"That can keep," Zack said, grasping Del's hand. "What're you doing here?"

"Furlough." Del grinned at him. "Things've ground to a standstill up at the bivouac. I've got a leave coming, so the captain told me to take it. I'm here for a month. Now, what happened to your cayuse?"

"Plenty of time to tell you," Zack returned. "The first thing I want to say is that you couldn't be more welcome."

CHAPTER IX

The Sleeper boys bent over their father, who sat with his back to a rock, his knees drawn up, a grimace twisting his sweating face. The flat of a horny hand pressed against the bloody cloth of his shirt at the right shoulder. He was cursing his offspring in a steady stream of obscene profanity while they tried to open the shirt and get at the undoubtedly serious wound.

In explosive anger, Purdy said, "Leggo of me, you sons of bitches, and make sure that bastard's dead!"

Neither of the sons looked drawn to the idea of venturing out through the gap and across open ground to see what their father had achieved in return for the price he had paid. Rip said viciously, "He'll keep, goddamn you! Get that hand down so we can see what he done to you!"

When working in harmony, they would lay down their lives for one another without giving it a thought. But when they fell out, they became more bitterly inimical than if no blood relationship existed. With an angry jerk, Frank ripped open the bloody shirt.

"You'll live," he muttered. "But you sure put yourself on the shelf for a while. Bullet missed your lung, or you'd be heavin' blood. But it sure busted that shoulder to hell." He lifted a hand when Purdy let go another string of curses. "Shut up. It was your own idea. You said you could handle him and wanted the pleasure."

Purdy stared down at the bloody, shattered shoulder himself. He still loosed profanity, which he interrupted to fume, "You puke-eatin' lunatics! Can't you get it through your heads this'll prove we bushwhacked him if he lives to make charges? You gotta see he's done for."

The sons stared at each other in sudden discernment. At Purdy's insistence, they had gone on with the cattle, leaving him to fall back. They knew where the Modocs kept a small band of stolen stuff that they drew on for food; it was on deeper in the lavas. It had been their aim to mix the cattle they had brought with that, making Captain Jack a present of them. In return they would confuse the issue of who had rustled in the devastated country up north, something the army would not look on with favor. It would get Zack off their backs and out of their way in future moves. Purdy had pointed that out, with considerable pride in himself, when he had first described the plan.

But the sons hadn't got too far away to hear the exchange of shots that told them Purdy hadn't pulled it off as slick as he had expected. They had let the cattle go and hurried back to find Purdy crawling out this end of the lava bore, dripping blood. Now, for the first time, they realized there could be consequences from Purdy's failure more serious than Zack's escape.

They ran to their horses, swung up, jerked their rifles up from boots, and went pounding into the notch. Once out of their father's sight, however, their pace slacked. They didn't leave the shadows of the gap until they were sure they would draw no fire themselves. Then they rode out to the dead horse.

"So it was a job Pa'd trust to nobody but himself!" Rip said with a snort. "He never even drawed blood — except from the cayuse. The old bastard's eyesight's failin' him."

"Sure messed it up," Frank agreed. "But he set Buckman afoot. We can catch him."

They picked up the sign without trouble and followed it south. Yet, for a reason neither cared to voice, they rode slowly, warily, vividly aware that Buckman would watch his back trail. If he observed pursuers, he would be the one to set up the next ambush.

"Hell," Rip said finally, "he's got the edge, even if he is afoot. One of us packin' a bullet's all we need right now. We'll have to claim Purdy and us jumped Injuns rustlin' on our range and they shot him in the ruckus, no matter what Zack says."

Frank nodded. Blaming Purdy helped cover their own disinclination to press a fight that had gone badly awry already. They turned back to where their father waited.

The bleeding and mounting pain had simmered Purdy down. He only stared up at them with dull eyes. He didn't do much but mutter when they told him Buckman had got away and what they would claim to account for his hurt shoulder. As the will in the sire diminished, the wills in the sons rose to dominate and thwart it in every possible way. They ripped his shirt into strips to bind the wound and brace the shoulder. They forced him back into his coat and cursed him blue when he fought against the pain of being lifted into the saddle. Then they rode out of the lavas, cutting a slant to the southwest. That would take them behind the Coyote Hills and home with little chance of meeting anyone.

It was dark when they reached Big S headquarters. Monk, left out of things as usual, heard them coming and was waiting outdoors in the warm night. He gaped at the slumped figure of his father. "Goddlemighty!" he breathed. "What happened? He run into Martin Dunes?"

Purdy roused enough to curse him silent. Then the three of them got him off the horse and into the house and on his bunk. Frank, being the oldest son, took up the reins of command, saying worriedly, "Rip, you got to bring a sawbones from Yreka. That's a mean hole in his shoulder. If it ain't treated right, he could be crippled for life."

Purdy opened his eyes to glare at him. "Forget it," he growled, "and get me the jug."

"Kee-rist, Pa," Frank argued, lifting the stone jug of raw whisky from under Purdy's bunk. "You could die of it."

"Lift me up, damn you, and shut your trap."

Frank complied, and his father took a long haul on the jug, caught his breath, and pulled thirstily again. When Frank reached for the jug to set it back on the floor, Purdy held onto it. Lying back, he let out a long sigh.

"You're fetchin' no sawbones," he said, "and you ain't tellin' a crazy yarn about Modocs' wingin' me. How much do you think folks'll swallow — even that woolhead sheriff in Yreka?"

Rip scowled. "What you gonna say, then?"

"Nothin'. I gotta lay low till this damn thing's healed up." The whisky was strengthening him, coloring his cheeks and bringing back his waspish will power. As it rose, the wills of his sons diminished. They looked at each other doubtfully but nodded their heads. "That damned Buckman," Purdy resumed. "His horse reared or he yanked it up right when I squeezed off my shot. Not only missed the son of a bitch. I give him a dead horse to fort behind, and me standin' there with just a screen of brush between us. Got me on the second shot. What could I do with a rifle and only a left hand?"

"Don't worry about him," Rip said. "We'll fix his wagon."

"Don't try anything on your own hook, damn you," Purdy snapped. "He never seen me. But if he goes to the sheriff on his guesswork, and the sheriff comes here, we'll be dancin' on air in Yreka."

"Hung?" Monk's jaw swung wide. "Say —
what happened?"

Rip gave him a thin grin. "We jumped some
Modocs rustlin' on us, and Pa was hit in the
ruckus. Huh, Frank?"

"That's right, Smack dab in the ruckus."

"Aw, hell." Monk turned sulkily away, a look
in his eyes promising that sooner or later he
would show them.

Purdy lay pulling on his whisky, now and then
groaning, again giving vent to strings of curses
directed at one or another of his sons, again at
something going through his mind. Frank fixed
a meal, and it had barely been eaten when Rip
swung his head in hard attention to something
outdoors. He had always had the keenest senses
of them, as good as an Indian's. After a moment
he said, "Horsebackers coming," and shoved up.

Monk shot a frightened look from face to face.
The mystery and what his father had said about
them hanging had got under his skin. Purdy was
too sodden by whisky and pain to notice anything. Rip and Frank caught up their rifles.

"You stay here," Frank snapped at Monk.

Outdoors, Rip took a long look at the two
approaching riders and muttered, "I think one's
Zack Buckman."

"Who's the other?"

"Dunno." Then, after a moment, he said,
"Jesus Christ. It's his brother. The one that
was supposed to be in the army."

Frank swore under his breath. "He's showed

up, too? What in hell?"

"They're checkin' to see who got hit, and that's all I know. What're we gonna tell 'em?"

"You let me talk," Frank said, frowning.

The Buckman brothers trotted in among the ranch buildings with no sign of nervousness and came right up to the two rifle-holding men who stood staring at them sullenly. Zack tipped a nod that somehow had the effect of pointing an accusing finger. Without greeting, he said brusquely, "Where's Purdy and the kid?"

"Monk's in the house," Frank said. "Somethin' you wanted to see him about?"

"No, I want to see Purdy."

"Well, he ain't home," Frank said. "Left for Virginia City a couple of days ago. We got kinfolks down that way. Pa reckoned on visitin' 'em a spell and seein' the elephant in Virginia. Anythin' in particular you wanted of him?"

"We got it." The two, thin grins on their faces, turned summarily and left.

They had ridden only a short distance when Rip growled, "By God, I'd like to salt their tails for 'em." He started to lift the rifle.

"Cut it out." Frank walked into the house and shook his father roughly. "Hey! You gotta get outta here Pronto."

Purdy seemed to have been dozing. He opened his eyes, lifted his head, then let it fall back. "Whatsa matter?" he said drunkenly.

"Zack Buckman and his brother just left. They know you're hit. They'll have the sheriff here

114

tomorrow, sure as hell. Layin' low won't do. You gotta get to a hide-out right now."

Purdy moaned.

"Come on," Frank insisted.

"Where to?"

"Where nobody can find you, goddamn it, and see you're shot up." Frank looked at Rip. "Fix grub and blankets. You, Monk. Go saddle our cayuses. Wish I'd thought to tell 'em you went to Virginia with him, because you got to stay with him. Guess we'll have to say you got an itch for the bright lights yourself and followed him down that way."

"Where'm I gonna stay with him?" Monk whined.

"That cave on Juniper Flat."

Monk shivered. He knew the place, one of the countless ice caves in the lava region. He was getting a real job, finally, but one devoid of the dash and derring-do craved by his vanity. He went sulkily outdoors.

The situation had sobered Purdy, whom Frank had coaxed to sit up. With a scowl, Purdy said, "Del Buckman, too? Hell, he's supposed to be in the army."

"Could've been paid off," Frank said. "I heard he was a short-timer."

"That puts another on our hands. Looks like I gotta hide out, but, damn your livers, don't you boys go off half-cocked. You keep me posted and get your orders from me. Hear?"

"We hear," Frank grunted. "We ain't fools

enough to stir up more hornets than you've stirred up already."

If there was anything Purdy prided himself on above all else, it was his ability to outsmart the world and wring from it what he wanted. Stung, he jerked up his head and said arrogantly, "One setback, and you chicken-livered whelps think we're licked! This ain't gonna stop us — anyhow not me!"

That was the kind of bluster that had always whipped up the boys' nerve and made them ready to take on all comers. Now it fell flat. Frank said, "Sure," to which Rip added, "You betcha." But they had tangled their string when they had decided to rustle in the Tule Lake country, and they had done it again trying to turn the tables on Zack Buckman, there in the edge of the lavas. Now, if they didn't get him hidden where he couldn't be found till he healed up, their father was a menace to them instead of the brainy leader he still wanted to pretend to be.

They all rode out into the night, striking an oblique angle across the south end of the Coyote Hills. This brought them down, about an hour later, on the juniper-dotted plateau that hugged the back side of the hills. The cave where they stopped presently was marked on the surface by no more than a gentle, brush-covered dome. It was well off the country's travelways and would escape detection by a stray traveler or a deliberate hunter unless he stumbled right up to it.

They got Purdy bedded down, left provisions and blankets for Monk; then Frank and Rip turned to leave.

"Hey!" Monk yelled when they gathered the reins of both the horses they weren't riding themselves. "You leave me a cayuse!"

"And have you rackin' all over the country?" Frank snorted. "Anyhow, there's nowhere to graze one without danger of it being seen. You stay with Purdy, hear? Don't go outside except to get wood for the fire, and that only in the dark. We'll bring more grub, and that'll be at night, too. So long, Purdy."

Purdy didn't answer. He had slipped into unconsciousness.

Monk's stomach felt like he had swallowed a cactus while he watched his brothers vanish into the far night. What made them so sure nobody would know of this place and think of it right off? He might have to stand off a sheriff's posse, or even Modocs, all by himself, which was a lot different from whamming lead at enemies with Purdy and Frank and Rip there to side him. He shivered and crept back into the cave. The hell with a fire tonight: he didn't feel like going out there scrounging for dead juniper wood and sagebrush. He got a blanket and covered himself, but he was too wound up to sleep.

Daylight began to change the color of his thoughts. Purdy was still unconscious, but quiet now instead of raving. Monk poked into the grub supply and got a couple of cold biscuits,

117

which he ate. He got himself a drink from the trickling stream that oozed out of a rock and ran down the slanting floor of the cave into its frigid depths. When he looked outside, the light was strong, and he felt braver. He went up on the surface, even though he had been told not to during the day.

He had been here before but without enough interest to take a good look at everything. Now he did. Off to the northeast he could see the lavas through the clear atmosphere of what promised to be another day of fine weather. Farther west was a mountain that let him fix the location of Van Bremer's ranch and the army camp, which he could not see. When he looked in the opposite direction, he discovered to his surprise that he could see Coyote Peak, which seemed right at hand in the clear air.

He stared at the peak with growing interest, getting his bearings. By damn. He was just across the hills from Forbidden Canyon. He realized this without fear that Martin Dunes might know of this cave or stumble onto him here. All he could think of was that only a mile or two of hills separated him from Wendy.

He went back into the cave. It didn't look as if Purdy had moved a limb all night. But he was alive, his shallow breathing making a faint rustling in dry nostrils. He looked pale and feverish, but Monk didn't know what to do about that or about the wound. His brothers hadn't told him. They wouldn't be back till night, and maybe not then, for there was grub enough to last a day or two more.

And, Monk realized, there was and would be no one to keep tabs on him. He tried to shake the temptation out of his head, but it stuck. It was tough having to sit there in the dark, cramped cave with the growing smell of sickness that came from his father. He stood it till noon, when he ate some more cold grub. Then, taking the rifle, he left.

He guided himself by the peak, and the juniper gave him plenty of cover until he reached taller timber. It surely felt good to be swinging along in the sunshine, even if it had to be on foot. Once he got a nearly perfect shot at a buck deer and had lifted the rifle to his shoulder before he remembered what a dangerous thing it would be to fire. Up in the ridges he began to work leftward, following the good ground, a sensation that always came up in him when he was on the prowl giving him pleasure. Almost before he knew it, he was stretched on his belly at the top of a rim of Forbidden Canyon, across from where he had spied when he used to come here from the Wagonwheel.

He was much closer now to the squaw man's cabin. Wendy and her father were down there in the yard, getting a little sunshine on themselves. Otherwise, they seemed to be just talking. Dunes was seated on a log, his back toward the rimrock, while Wendy stood facing him. She had her hands behind her, and Monk's breath caught at the way the yellow light fell on her breasts. She was laughing, the first time he had ever watched her when she wasn't working at something, her face looked tight as an Indian's. Her merriment surprised Monk. He had always thought of old Dunes as having a face that would clabber milk. It was odd to think of him making a joke.

Monk grinned to himself. His father, their predicament, and his responsibility in it had been wiped from his mind. He slid the rifle forward and lined its sights on the hollow of Dunes' shoulders. One squeeze of the trigger, and the old watchdog would be out of the way. Then the girl — ! Monk felt the hot oils of lust flow through him and concentrate in an intolerable pressure in his belly. He pulled the rifle back beside him with effort.

It was well that he hadn't given in to his surging temptation. In a moment both Duneses turned their heads to look down the canyon. Shifting his own gaze, Monk frowned. Zack Buckman was riding in, bold as if he lived in Forbidden Canyon. Wendy didn't run like a scared doe, either. She stood there calmly while Zack rode up to them. It was the first time Monk had hated Zack with a positive and personal antagonism. What was Dunes doing, letting him come around the girl, when he had driven Monk Sleeper off at the point of a gun? Zack was no different from any other man.

Monk left reluctantly, thwarted, angry, and

more bent than ever on getting his hands on the girl. He was within easy watching distance, and the chance would come.

He was halfway to Juniper Flat before it dawned on him that Zack could not have gone to Yreka for the sheriff after he and his brother were at the Sleeper place the night before. It didn't seem likely that the other Buckman would go in, when he was pretty much a stranger in the country. No, even if he didn't believe the Virginia City yarn, Zack knew Purdy was too smart to be where he could be found and examined for a fresh gun wound. That was some comfort. Monk still had no taste for being required to fight off a posse to keep his father and brothers from dancing on thin air.

CHAPTER X

Zack had just told Martin Dunes of his experiences at the edge of the lava fields, hoping that their common enmity of the Sleeper clan would yet turn into a common bond between himself and Wendy's father. The ambush had also served as an excuse to come here, averting for a while a showdown on whether Dunes would permit a friendship with Wendy. He hadn't dismounted because there had been no invitation to do so.

"Purdy's either hiding out," Zack concluded, "or he's dead, with his whelps not able to admit it without admitting their part in that bushwhacking."

"He's alive," Dunes said. His manner still was neither friendly nor hostile. "They wouldn't have said he'd gone visitin' if it wasn't possible for him to come back. He's holed up, but with all the places he could do that in, it'd take an army to find him."

Zack nodded his agreement, and that finished his business with Dunes. He looked at Wendy, who was listening quietly, glancing his way now and then with veiled eyes. "Do you know Dora Agee, Wendy?" he asked.

She was startled. "I've seen her a few times."

"There's going to be a wedding," Zack went

on. "Dora and my brother Del. He come home on a furlough yesterday and they set the date last night. Thought you might like to go with me. She said she'd sure like to have you there."

Dunes could not be too stupid to understand the expression that flooded his daughter's face. He met the father's scowling eyes, daring him to state again that she was not lonely and not starved for the things his way of life had denied her.

"It's to be the middle of June," Zack resumed relentlessly. "Right after Del gets paid off. But Dora's got plenty to do before then. She wants to make her a wedding dress and clothes for their honeymoon. It'd be nice if you could get acquainted and help her. She mentioned it herself. Why don't you ride over to her place with me one of these — ?"

"Stop it!" Dunes said in exploding fury.

Zack laid a flat stare on the man's hot eyes. "Never really believed your claim, did you?" he murmured. "Would you like to do that, Wendy?"

Wendy glanced at her father, then shook her head. "I don't reckon so," she said in a dull voice. "Thanks kindly."

Zack touched his hat to her and turned his horse down the canyon.

Maybe he had let her in for trouble with her father, he thought. Dunes might curry her hard for betraying what he would consider a weakness and disloyalty. Yet somehow Zack doubted that

Dunes was that kind. He had gambled every-thing on his hunch that there was a true father hidden somewhere beneath that bitterness.

The days following went fast. There wasn't a sign of Frank and Rip Sleeper, and Zack and Del put in long hours riding their range. They dug out springs to make them impound more water for the stock. They built catch basins in gullies to capture and hold the rains of the next winter. They got ready for the calf branding that would start around the first of May if circum-stances permitted.

In the evenings Del rode over to see Dora while Zack smoked his pipe in the pleasant weather that endured. Zack thought a lot about Wendy, but he knew it would be unwise to go back too soon to Forbidden Canyon. He had made his plants to take root or die, and he had to allow time for one or the other to happen.

In the last week of March, Zack turned the cares of the ranch and the menaced Wagonwheel over to Del and made a pack trip to Yreka for supplies. Going in, he stopped at Van Bremer's ranch to catch up on the news. Van Bremer had heard from Ernie Yost. The surgeons at Fort Klamath had saved his leg, and he was on the mend.

Zack learned, also, that Wheaton had been re-placed by another colonel of the 1st Regiment, Alvan C. Gillem, as commanding officer of the increased forces being mustered against the Mo-docs. The command would be brought to a strength of nearly a thousand men by the addition of three companies of the 21st Infantry, two of the 12th Infantry, and four batteries of the 4th Artillery, all of which were on their way from various posts in the West.

But all of that had been put in suspension, for the Indian Department had asked the War Department to hold fire. "Maybe you don't remember A. B. Meacham," Van Bremer said. "He was a little before your time. But he used to be Indian Superintendent for Oregon, and it was him who talked Captain Jack into going back to the reservation the other time. Jack liked Meacham, so the bigwigs figure Meacham can persuade him again. He's been back in Washington, and they're sending him out to try."

That ended Zack's hope of the Indian trouble's being settled before Purdy Sleeper had recovered from his wound. Gruffly, he said. "What do you think of Meacham's chances?"

"Zero," Van Bremer said with a snort. "There's been so much killing, the white folks would never let those Modocs off without half of 'em being hung. Don't think Jack don't know that, too."

Gillem, the new colonel, likewise took a dim view of Meacham's prospects There was talk that he planned to move the army base over to the west edge of the lavas to make it more convenient for the negotiations — and, afterward, for the military effort Gillem still expected to have to make.

In Yreka Zack bought supplies enough to load two packhorses, for he didn't know when he might get to make the trip again. The choice of articles designed solely to please a woman was limited, however. He searched the town before he settled an a hand mirror, comb, and brush set in imitation amber. He bought it, spent the night in town, and the next day rode back to the Wagonwheel.

He had meant to wait longer, but the following afternoon found him on the way to Forbidden Canyon, riding with a package under his arm. He had hoped to catch Wendy alone, but Dunes was there, as if he had taken to riding herd on her. Then Zack noticed that they had just dressed a deer that hung in the shade of the cabin. Both had come around front while he rode up the canyon. Dunes' sealed countenance told him nothing. But Zack hoped that the hint of excitement in Wendy's eyes meant she was glad to see him.

He decided to ignore the etiquette of such an occasion and swung down without invitation and trailed the reins of the horse. Wendy's eyes were on the package, but he supposed she was only curious, for she would know little of the gallantries a man showed the girl he was courting. Unless — for the first time he wondered if she had Indian suitors, if his persistence might crowd her father into forcing her to marry one of them. The thought was appalling, not because he considered Indians inferior, as so many white people did. It was just the idea of her marrying anybody but himself.

He extended his offering, saying casually, "Seen something in Yreka, the other day, I thought mebbe you'd like, Wendy. I was coming over this way anyhow, so I thought I'd stop by with it."

Her eyes widened, and she looked up at his face. Her father betrayed no expression when she turned a questioning glance on him.

"Go on, take it," Zack encouraged.

Her hands, long, brown and strong, grasped the package uncertainly. He wondered if it was the first she had seen wrapped in store paper and string. He pulled out his jackknife and cut the string. She had trouble getting off the heavy paper. The set had been put in a shoe box by the storekeeper. She lifted one corner of the lid and peeked in as if she expected something to jump at her. Then she removed the lid, and he heard the intake of her breath. She knew what it was for, all right.

"Better'n lookin' in the crick," Zack said, grinning. "Go on. See what a pretty girl you are."

Dunes muttered, "You're teachin' her vanity."

"She needs a little. Bad."

Wendy was looking in the mirror with an expression of awe. Then, her face twisting, she handed the set back. "Thank you, but — I can't —" She turned and fled into the cabin.

Dunes' seamy brown face was locked even tighter than before.

"It cost her a lot to give this back, mister," Zack said angrily. "And you know it."

"You oughtn't to have brought it. You oughtn't to have started comin' here."

"Does she think the same?"

"What makes you so sure what she thinks?"

"I'm young, too, Martin. And nothin' ever turned me sour on life."

Dunes scuffed the ground with a moccasined foot, staring down. Zack put the presents on the chopping block by the door. "She wants 'em pretty bad, so I'll be leavin' 'em. You can bust 'em with the ax, if you want." He turned to mount his horse.

"Wait." Dunes started to say something belligerent, then shook his head, and his voice came soft. "Don't bring torment to her."

"I think you mean torment to you."

Dunes said nothing. Zack swung up and rode off.

That evening Zack confided in Del, getting it all off his chest. "It's a puzzling setup," he said in conclusion. "I could be doing a rotten, mean thing."

"Not if you love the girl," Del retorted. "Do you?"

"Guess so." Zack looked at his brother. "But I'm makin' trouble between 'em. What if she don't and can't ever feel the same way about me?"

"If she don't or can't, you can't make her unhappier than she already is. And Dunes has got no right to be unhappy, as long as our intentions toward her are decent." Del sighed. "It's sure a shame. The lord only knows what effect his raisin' has had on her, if she'll ever throw it all off."

"With me meddlin' on a gamble that he's the man I figure he was before Purdy Sleeper wrecked his life."

"It sure is a gamble," Del admitted. "I can't help you there."

Zack knew that things weren't too happy for Del and Dora at present. Del's furlough would be up in a few more days, and the odds were great that he would have one more trip to make into the lava beds before he saw Dora again. That was the ghost that haunted them now, even if they talked with stubborn confidence of wedding bells in June.

Zack and Del were having their noon meal the next day when Hollis Brown rode in from the south side of Hub Lake. "Purdy's back on Big S." Hollis said worriedly. "I was in Yreka and come back by way of his place, and he was settin' on the porch, feeble-like. And, Zack, that bastard's got a sagged shoulder he never had when he disappeared. Handles it stiff and careful, even though he tried not to with me there. Monk's there, too, and I sure ain't restin' easy with that wolf pack back together. I'm next door to the range they took off the Mintos."

"You are," Zack agreed, "and I won't throw

you off guard by trying to make it look better for you than it is. You're in danger. We all are. Look what they tried on me in the lavas." He shook his head. "Wish you could hire a man somewhere to stay with you till Ernie gets back. I heard at Van Bremer's that he's still got two legs and is mending. He'll be here soon as he can make it. You can count on that."

"I know. I only wish I could count on being alive when he does."

"Well, you're warned," Zack said. "And that's an advantage Johnny Minto never had."

Brown left, and after a moment Del said, "Hell of a time for me to have to go back. I'll worry more about Dora here, if Monk's showed up again, than about what I'll have to do up there. He manhandled her a while back. I knew something troubled her and worked it out finally. She come within an inch of not getting away from him."

"I thought so," Zack said. "Wendy told me he spied on her till Martin caught and threatened him."

"It's all I can do," Del reflected, "to keep from riding over there and taking care of him. But I can't, with nothing but Dora's claim that he molested her. It would give the Sleepers an excuse, as the injured parties, to bring their sneak war out in the open."

Zack agreed. The thought of the degenerate kid's putting his hands on any woman was revolting. Now Wendy was far more than just a woman to him, and he knew Del felt the same way about Dora.

Del left three days later, once more wearing his chevrons and yellow-striped pants, once more the hardened campaigner not yet able to call his life his own. His departure was nearly as depressing to Zack as to Dora, leaving a void that could be filled only with work.

Zack threw himself into it, and when there was not enough work actually required, he made it, cutting wood on the slopes of Pistol Peak and yarding it out to dry, cutting poles for future corrals and fences. Then the false spring of February collapsed as March grew on. Again clouds hung for days over the Wagonwheel, sometimes loosing heavy rains that kept him restlessly pacing the floor at home, with too much time for thought.

It was after a day and night of such stormy weather that Zack awakened with a resolve he had not formed consciously to venture another visit to Forbidden Canyon. It was born, he learned, of the promise of restored good weather, which he observed when he looked outdoors. He was not the only one being tormented by pent-up energies, he knew, in this lull that was not peace. It was time or past time something happened again, and his first concern in that respect had become Wendy.

CHAPTER XI

Monk was on upper Coyote Creek, excitement boiling in him, for — a thing he would not have dreamed of doing a short while ago — he was going down into Forbidden Canyon along a trail worn by Martin Dunes and the Indians Dunes ran with. New as the idea was, it had burned like a brand in Monk's brain ever since he got it, forging itself into a decision during the last couple of days, while he was cooped up on Big S by the stormy weather. When he had awakened this morning to a cloudless sky, he had known that his day had come.

He carried his rifle and moved at a swift, skulking gait down a well-worn footpath. The horse he had ridden from home was back on the bench, since the noise it made could get him killed. Now he slipped along with assurance, following the creek toward the lower ground, for his plan couldn't miss. His own folks wouldn't catch onto it, even. He had told them, when he left the ranch, that he was going the other way, west onto the Shasta plateau, to see if he could knock down an antelope.

In the last brush before the canyon door, Monk halted for a look before he went any farther. He had grown acquainted with the setup and routine here during his hours of watching from the rim while he lived in the ice cave with Purdy. There had been nearly a week, at first, when Purdy was either out of his head or too weak to notice or care whether his son was there. Monk had gone every day to the rim of Forbidden Canyon. After Purdy had got better but not healed enough to go home, Monk had contented himself with slipping off at night to perch himself on the rim and moon over the girl asleep in the cabin below, his desire for her fanned by the fact that he had seen Zack Buckman there and by his determination to beat Zack to her.

He had learned the ways of the Duneses in the daylight visits. The old man stuck pretty close to home these days, but he had his habits, and every day about this time he went down the canyon and looked at some traps he had set along the lower creek. From the rim, a while ago, Monk had seen him leave. Now Monk took another long look to make sure nothing had brought him back early. The space around the cabin was empty, and the girl was, he knew, indoors. He went on silently.

He could be quiet as an Indian himself, and he made it to the open door without being heard. His heart was slamming, but with expectation, not fear. Wendy was seated at a table, three-fourths turned from him. She was looking into a hand mirror and brushing her pretty hair. She did it slowly, like she enjoyed it. He watched her smile at herself.

Then she seemed to catch sight of him in the

reflection as she moved the mirror. He saw her freeze. She drew a breath before she turned slowly on the chair. Her shoulders pulled back, and her mouth dropped ajar. He had the rifle trained right between the pretty mounds on her chest.

"Don't let out a peep," he warned.

He thought for a moment that she would defy him and scream, which would liven things up for him. But she changed her mind and said with the contempt an Indian could manage when he was sore, "What do you want?"

"You. Come on."

She just sat there as if she didn't believe what was happening to her.

He cocked the rifle, and its click convinced her that he meant business. She got up slowly, her cheeks drained. He never moved the gun barrel an inch, motioning instead with his head. "Get walkin'. Outside and up the crick."

"What — what for?"

She was on to things better than he thought for a girl who had been kept out of them most of her life. She knew what he wanted of her all right. He saw her catch a quick breath when he grinned. She came toward him with faltering steps, and he backed up so she could pass by him and get ahead. She turned up the creek, walking as if her moccasins were made out of lead. Monk flung a quick look down the creek. The space down there was still empty. Then he hurried after her.

They were halfway up the trail before he told her to stop. She did, and then turned to him, her eyes full of hatred. She said coldly, "Pa'll kill you."

"No, he won't. Now or ever."

He tied her firmly to a tree with the catch-rope he had left there on his way down. He gagged her with his bandanna. "You're gonna be my squaw," he announced. "Long as I want you."

Her eyes flashed fire, but she couldn't say anything.

"I know a little place," he said, "where I'll keep you. They won't ever find you. Just me, when I feel like it. I'll come there. You won't get away because you're gonna be tied up when I ain't there. I figured it all out." Her eyes angered him, and he said hotly, "Think you're too good, you damned squaw? You get highfalutin' with me, and I won't feed you. I'll let you starve to death."

It was queer how she managed to make him feel gawky and half-grown just from stiffening her slim body and staring at him. He turned and hurried down the trail.

He had picked his spot long since, and he went to it at once, a big round boulder that lay half-buried beside the creek and had brush all around it. He had to bend only a little to cover himself and yet see the front of the cabin and the trail down the creek. It was a moment he had hungered for ever since the time Dunes caught him on the rim and threatened to geld him.

He didn't know whether he had waited a long time or it just seemed that way when he saw the buckskinned figure of the squaw man far down the canyon and walking his way. In spite of himself, Monk swallowed. There was no need to be boogery. He couldn't miss. When Dunes reached the cabin door, he would be only fifty-sixty feet away.

Dunes came on unworriedly, covering ground in his long-legged stride. Sure of his supremacy, Monk calmed down. He knew Dunes would reach the door of the cabin, lean his rifle against the wall, and pick up an armload of split wood to take into the house. That was one thing Dunes hadn't learned from the Indians: doing work a squaw should do. Monk watched him do exactly as expected, and the instant there was no rifle in his hand, Monk fired. The man was spun half around, knocked back so that he was tilted against the wall, when Monk shot again. He had slid to the ground before his body received the third and last shot. Monk went bounding up the trail.

When Zack rode out toward the Coyote Hills, he knew that the day — and maybe several of them — would contribute to the advent of spring. The smell of rain-scrubbed earth rose on the warming air. Except for a few straggling tags of clouds, the sky was a clean, bright blue from the Cascades to the far Warners. His horse scared up sage hens from the basin floor. The jaws of the Coyote Creek gorge, as he moved toward them, had the sharpness of an ax cleft in the washed, brilliant air.

The ride through the unsunned gorge reminded him that winter had not entirely decamped. Coyote Creek ran cold in its scabby channel beside the trail, and the fractured walls of rock bulged in oppressively. Then Zack came out in Forbidden Canyon, with the foreboding that had prompted this visit returned to him. There was no one in view around the Dunes cabin, which he could see for quite a distance. He rode on in at a trot.

He was nearly to the corner of the cabin before he realized that the object on the ground, flung out beyond the woodpile, was part of a man's buckskin-clad leg. With a constricted throat, Zack swung down from the saddle and hurried forward and looked down at Martin Dunes, who was sprawled in a bloody heap between the woodrick and cabin door.

He gasped, "Martin — what — !" Then he looked around hastily, strode to the door and glanced inside. He yelled "Wendy!" before his benumbed mind realized that if she was anywhere near and able to do it, she would have been with her father. Dropping to a hunker, he put a hand on Dunes' shoulder.

It was warm. The gravity of the wounds told Zack that the thing couldn't have happened very long before.

"Martin!" he said desperately, gently shaking.

"What happened, man? Wendy — where is she? Martin, you've got to tell me!"

The first real evidence that the man still breathed came with a low moan that stirred up from his blood-soaked chest. Dunes' lips worked inanely, then grew still. His eyes opened slightly, heavily, but there didn't seem to be life and consciousness behind them.

Zack said in low-voiced insistency, "Was it the Sleepers?"

The lips contorted and breath came out with no sound. After an agonizing moment, the breath began to make ragged, barely audible words.

"Must . . . of been. Help her . . . Buckman . . ."

Monk, Zack thought, and felt a deep sickness. "You didn't see who did it?"

"No. From the . . . crick brush. Tell her . . . it's canceled . . . what I made her promise. She belongs . . . to your . . . world . . . Buckman . . ."

The head rolled suddenly. The will that had kept Dunes alive was used up. The effort of regaining consciousness, of speaking, had drained away the last of his life. Zack felt of a limp wrist, let it drop and sprang to his feet.

His heart nearly stopped when he saw the combing set on the table. It looked like Wendy had been using it when this thing had started. There was no sign of a struggle indoors. Then, outside the door, he saw the tracks of riding boots larger than his own. The man had forced Wendy to come out to him. The rifle leaning against the wall suggested that Dunes had been waylaid afterward. The tracks that pointed up the creek would be easy to follow. The killer hadn't expected there to be anyone besides Dunes to track him before another rain washed the bootprints out.

Debating, Zack decided to take his horse, ran back to mount, then started up the creek. He noticed the rock where the murderer had forted up but went on without stopping. He could see the prints of small moccasins. A killing rage roared in him.

He found tracks at the base of a tree that told him Wendy had been lashed there while her abductor went back to do his dirty work, figuring it would eliminate the one chance of immediate pursuit. That made the girl the prime objective, which again pointed to Monk Sleeper and his insane lust.

On the bench above the upper canyon, Zack found tracks and droppings of a waiting horse. His fury mounted when he realized that the killer had chosen to ride and make Wendy walk ahead of him. At the end of a rope, at the point of a gun. The sign ran on to the northwest, but Zack hadn't expected Monk to take his prize home. An open murder and the abduction of a woman were things even Purdy wouldn't stand for, not from decency, but from wisdom. Monk had some hiding place in mind. Zack rode as swiftly as he could follow the sign, painfully aware that if he lost it, it could cost him excruciating time. He didn't dare to think of what might already have happened and forced himself to concentrate on the immediate requirements of his problem.

The man he stalked seemed well acquainted with the area they were in. Sometimes the trail followed a ridge for a distance, plunging down across a canyon, and then reversed itself on the next summit, bearing over to the northwest. Finally it slanted down the slope under thin pine, and Zack realized that it would come out on the open plateau above Juniper Flat. On the plateau, where sun and wind dried things out more rapidly, the recent rain helped him, for the earth was still soft. But the forward country seemed completely empty. He wondered if Monk had stolen the girl with an idea of taking her out of the country, aware that his own family would rise up against him for such heedless folly.

A mile later Zack saw a low, brushy lava dome, knew what it was, and that he had reached the end of the trail. He pulled down, seeing no one. The sooner he let Monk know somebody was hot on his trail, the better were Wendy's chances. After lifting the rifle, he sent a shot whistling over the dome, its cracking sound rolling after it. That would help. The degenerate's bullying cowardice had been proved already.

Zack went in fast, bent in the saddle and cutting a curve that brought him in at the side of the crown. He flung himself from the saddle the second the horse slid to a stop, then scrambled on top of the dome above the cave entrance. A Big S horse, Monk's favorite, was hidden in the trough below him.

Zack yelled, "Monk, you let that girl walk out of there! Hear? If she's all right I'll turn you over to the sheriff for a fair trial! If she's not all right, by God, I'll make you die the slowest, hardest way I can find to kill you! I mean every word of it!"

There was no response.

"I'm gonna count to ten, Monk; then the bargain's off," Zack shouted. "You don't have a ghost of a chance to get away with it. I can hold you there till you starve or kill you when you come out! One, two, three . . ." There was still only silence below him, so profound that he could hear the breeze in the sage. "Four, five, six . . . !"

"I ain't hurt her!" Monk yelled back.

"Send her out, Monk! Seven, eight, nine . . . !"

"Hold it! She's comin'!"

Zack shut his eyes for a second when Wendy, pale and looking sick, stepped out of the darkness below him. But she didn't seem to have been roughed up. Sure of himself, Monk might have taken his time about reaping the fruits of his ungodly effort.

And then Monk followed, with his rifle trained

on her back. Without looking up, he yelled, "You ain't so damned smart, Buckman! Move down where I can see you, or she gets it through the gizzard!"

Zack sucked in a breath, his memory of Martin Dunes proof that Monk would kill her without compunction if he thought it would help his chances. Zack fought the temptation to shoot him in the back, the way her father had died. But that might not stop the pervert from firing a shot that would be fatal to Wendy, the way the rifle was aimed.

"Goddamn it, get down here!" Monk bawled. "I can count, too. One, two, three —"

Wendy halted him by swinging disdainfully around and facing him. She looked up at Zack. "Don't," she called. "It won't help me. He'd only kill you."

"He harmed you?"

She shook her head.

"Come on, Buckman!" Monk yelled. "Four, five, six . . . !" He faltered. Wendy was staring at him with a magnificent contempt, a stinging detestation. "You turn around!" he shouted at her, making a stabbing motion with the rifle. "Don't look at me like that, you damned squaw!"

Wendy lifted her eyes to Zack and smiled.

It was too much for Monk. With a sudden leap, he got beyond her, turned so he could cover them both, but with his aim still centered on Wendy. His face was twisted in desperation, and he began to back away. At the top of the slanting trough, he whistled. His horse turned its head, then its body, and walked up to him in trained obedience. But not once did Monk take the rifle off Wendy, permitting Zack to risk a shot.

"Now toss down your gun, Buckman," Monk ordered. His fear had him panting, and it was the wholly dangerous fear of a beast at bay.

Even Zack hadn't noticed that Wendy was inching backward with slow, imperceptible movements of her moccasined feet. The first he knew was that suddenly she moved and wasn't there, for the black cave mouth had swallowed her. His target lost or confused, Monk knew better than to waste time on a blind shot at her. He elevated his aim and stabbed a shot at Zack, who sensed it in time to shift sideways. Zack shot even as he heard the snap of a bullet passing his head. He saw Monk stagger a step down the slope of the trough, then pitch forward. The man landed in an all-gone spill.

A moment later Zack had slid down to where he lay and grew sure Monk Sleeper would do no more harm in the world. Wendy had come out of the cave and walked up to him.

"Pa?" she faltered. "He's . . . dead?"

Zack nodded. "I'm sorry, Wendy."

She went on to the top while Zack walked into the cave. It took a moment for his eyes to adjust to the bad light; then he saw signs of a great deal of camping and living there. Sure. This was where Monk had hidden out with Purdy. Monk must have meant to keep Wendy a prisoner here for his foul purpose. Zack turned and stared at the body. He would load it on the Big S horse and send it home, returning to Purdy the monster created by Purdy's own example.

When he walked up to the surface, the Big S horse was gone and so was Wendy. He saw her on the animal, moving quietly, trying to get away without his knowing it. She was heading not for Forbidden Canyon but northeast.

Toward the lava beds.

"Wendy!" he yelled through cupped hands. "Hey — ! Wait!"

Her answer was to dig her heels into the horse's sides and send it driving onward.

He raced around to his own horse and swung up, then went after her. But there had been reason why that horse had been Monk's favorite. It was fast. It kept gaining even at Zack's hardest pace, and if Wendy heard his shouts and pleas she deafened herself to them. At the edge of the lavas he gave up.

He knew now what the promise had been — from which, on his dying breath, her father had released her. Dunes had told her where to go if something happened to him binding her to it, if it was not her own desire that now drove her.

CHAPTER XII

The Modoc stood blended in the rocky shadows of a sawtooth formation that flanked the trough linking the stronghold and Tule Lake. His hair, skin and clothing all but dissolved his figure in the monotone of lava slag and gray sky. He was Kientepoos, Captain Jack, square-set of body, ugly of countenance, a savage whose brain burned with the desire for freedom and whose heart was heavy once more with despair.

His eyes, which were all that moved in his face, were on a rowboat, well out in the lake, that moved slowly eastward, bearing an officer and an armed escort. There had been many such boats, in recent days, shuttling between the army camp, which had moved from Van Bremer's ranch to the foot of the bluffs on the lavas' western edge, and the outpost on the east side of the beds, where Captain Bernard had been reinforced by the command of Captain Mason. All this was going on, Jack mused, while the authorities insisted that they only wanted to talk peace with the Modocs and bring an end to the war.

Jack's attention narrowed on the lake shore below him, where a young woman after water was waiting in hiding for the boat to pass. She was a slender, pretty woman who had come to him three weeks ago and, since then, had borne her share of the women's work in the stronghold. So complete was her devotion to the hopeless cause she had embraced, it was hard to remember that she was a white woman. The boat moved on behind a point, and Jack watched her fill her vessels. His people had told him of her arrival and what had prompted it, but he had never spoken to her. He turned and made his way down across the tumbled rock.

He was standing in the wide, deep trough when she came along from the lake, moving light and strong with her burden. His face did not change, and he was unsure of why he felt a desire to speak with her now. She stopped respectfully, her head tipped and her gaze on the ground at his feet.

He said in the Modoc tongue, which he knew she spoke, "Are they treating you well?" She nodded, not looking up at his eyes. She had joined Hooker Jim's people, from which had come the woman who had been like her mother. "My heart is heavy that they killed Martin Dunes," he resumed. "He was our friend." Again she nodded. "But you shouldn't have come here, little one. Soon we will all be dead or prisoners."

She raised her eyes, then, and met his. She said in a monotone, "You are my people."

He stared at her, more strongly moved than his face expressed. His curt nod dismissed her, and she went on toward the stronghold. He went down to the lake, empty now of soldier messengers.

Since the battle nearly three months before, he had temporized day by day, maintaining an uneasy control over his people, extending sun by sun the period in which they could remain free men. That could not continue much longer, in spite of what Schonchin John, Curly Doctor, Hooker Jim and their followers maintained. Military might would not end it primarily, but nature herself would. For two weeks there had been no rain, and soon no more could be expected until autumn, and the cisterns in the lavas would dry up. Then the army would need do no more than drive in and seize this lake shore, and the doom of the Modocs would be certain.

The only alternative to that and abject surrender was surrender now, while he still had a little power to bargain.

His mind went back over the many weeks since the battle. The complete rout of the army then had, in a sense, doomed the Modocs, for in most of them it had engendered a stubborn, wholly false sense of omnipotence. The hotbloods, whose records would guarantee their being hung if they surrendered or were captured, had rallied more strongly than ever to Curly Doctor and his confederate, Schonchin John. The miracle of the fog had convinced them that the Great Spirit was with them, that Curly Doctor's influence with him was absolute. Had the medicine man not brought them victory? And, later, a herd of cattle and calves that had appeared mysteriously in the southern lavas for them to eat? Could he not bring water if they were cut off from the lake? Could he not protect them to the natural end of their lives?

And there had been another element to contend with — those not trusting to the mystic powers to save them, yet also set against surrender. These had simply lost faith in the agreements of the white people. Believing themselves doomed to die, no matter what, they were solidly against giving up this stronghold, where they could sell their lives dearly and with the dignity of Modocs.

The white people, Jack thought, were doing little to prove their trustworthiness to these more realistic ones among his people. Some six weeks ago A. B. Meacham had arrived at army headquarters. With him was General Canby, chief of all the soldiers in the Northwest, and others who comprised what they called a peace commission. They had sent in a squaw man, Bob Whittle, and his Indian wife and asked to meet with Jack at the edge of the lavas.

Jack had agreed to meet them if they would come without the hated soldiers, whose presence would only inflame his people further beyond reason. This Meacham had refused, and weeks had passed in such futile attempts at negotiation. Meacham had employed as his agents Jack's cousin Winema and her white husband Frank

Riddle, then Jack's friend John Fairchild, and finally his old friend from Yreka days, Elija Steele.

The talks between emissaries had reduced even Jack's hopes of a settlement that he could persuade his people to accept. He secured an offer of amnesty, finally, but in return he and his people were to go as prisoners to Angel Island in San Francisco Bay and there remain confined until a reservation had been found for them. Jack had agreed even to that if the reservation would be on their beloved Lost River, but that had been denied to them.

The longer Jack resisted, the sterner grew the peace commission's demands. The promise of general amnesty was qualified, with the demand made that Hooker Jim and other known murderers be given up for trial. This was something that even Jack rejected with all his heart. The army camp moved in close to the lavas then. Soldiers in great numbers had joined it. A company of Warm Springs scouts, old enemies of the Modocs, was on its way to help defeat them, if it came again to war.

Then, surprisingly, there had been a meeting that had promised to get somewhere. Steele, Winema, Riddle, and Fairchild had come into the lavas, bringing with them a newspaper reporter, William Atwood, and Jack had received them personally. Jack had offered, in return for a guarantee of amnesty for all of them, to go to a reservation at Yainax, knowing in his heavy heart that it was the best he could hope to achieve. If not Yainax, then Hot Creek, or even the lava beds. No white men wanted them.

Steele's comments had suggested that this might be considered by the commissioners, which had brought Schonchin John to his feet.

"Why for they send you?" the dissident had demanded furiously of the emissaries. "Why for the big peace mans no come and make promises? They let you make promises! Then they can say they no tell you to and no keep 'em!"

"Why," Steele had said, taken aback, "we're only trying to narrow the issues to what will be talked about at the big council. That's how it's done when people who have been at war make peace."

"You tell Meacham to come here!" Schonchin John had shouted. "You tell Canby! Then *we* tell *them* what we will talk about!"

Steele and Fairchild had exchanged uneasy glances. Three faces out of four around them had shown a sharing of Schonchin John's sentiments. The emissaries had been in danger and had known it, and that had included Winema, who had interpreted when necessary. Steele had temporized, suggesting that the meeting be postponed until the next day, when heads would be cooler. Jack had given them the protection of his own cave that night, but the next day had shown no cooling off in the dissident faction. Steele and his party had gotten away only on Steele's promise to send in the peace commissioners themselves.

Why had Schonchin John and his supporters demanded that, when they were not willing to talk surrender to any man on any terms? Jack thought he knew. Meacham was the man who had persuaded Jack to take them to the reservation before. Canby was the soldier chief whose orders, in the winter, had driven them again from Lost River. Another commissioner, L. S. Dyer, was the Klamath Indian agent. The fourth, Reverend Eleazar Thomas, was a sunday Doctor from Petaluma, California, with dreams of a life for the Indians so pious that no Indian could endure it. . . .

Jack grew aware of someone's coming and turned to see Scarface Charley emerge from the trough and walk toward him. Waiting until his one reliable lieutenant had come up to him, Jack said quietly, "Is something wrong?"

"Your cousin Winema," Charley said. "She has come alone, Kientepoos, and she wants to see you alone. She's waiting out there." He motioned toward the great sea of rock to the south west.

"See me?" Jack said, frowning. "What about?"

"She brings a message to you from the peace commissioners. They know that most of your people will fight to the death. That only a few are for making peace. They want you to bring those who want peace out of the rocks. They will protect you and such people while it is done."

"I will not talk to her about that in secret," Jack returned. "I do not hide what is in my heart. I will not hide what I do. Take her to my cave and call the people together."

"Tell everybody?" Charley said, frowning. "Schonchin John — Curly Doctor — Hooker Jim — they will not agree, Kientepoos."

"They might agree to let the ones who want to leave do so." Jack shook his head tiredly. "At least the women and children and the old people who had done nothing they could be hanged for."

"You would not go?"

Jack shook his head again. "And neither would you, while some of us must fight to the death or be hanged."

Scarface Charley nodded his agreement with that. He turned and walked swiftly away, going back into the stronghold. Jack stood on the lake shore a while longer, wondering what had brought this about. Apparently the peace commissioners had given up hope and turned the problem back over to the army. That would account for the increased signaling between the signal station on top of the bluff and the army outpost to the east, and for the increased boat trips of the army couriers.

They were offering him and those who saw the hopelessness of their plight a chance to escape the attack they were about to launch. An attack that Curly Doctor might not be able to confuse and defeat with a spectral fog, that might rob them of water that Curly Doctor could not restore. Jack thought of his wives and children, of the young white woman with the deep unhappiness in her eyes, of the old people who were wearing out their short days and frail bodies in the rocks. He yearned to send them all out to safety and peace. So would all his braves, if they were the proud warriors they boasted of being instead of defiant outlaws with their backs to the wall. He turned and walked in toward the camp.

The central area of the stronghold was filling with people hurrying in from various points in the rocks. Jack strode through the throng, ignoring the searching, sometimes hopeful looks on their faces. He saw his opposers in a knot to one side. They looked excited, angry and stubborn. He entered his cave to find Winema waiting there, a comely, rotund woman who many times had proved her courage, never more than in this solitary mission for the sake of the people she had left but not forgotten. Her face was broad, her nose strong and straight, her eyes wide apart and intelligent.

"Kientepoos," she said urgently, "you do not understand. It is you and the people who support you in your wish for peace they want to come out."

"It is they who do not understand, cousin," Jack corrected in a weary voice. "That the only way I will divide my people is between the warriors and those who are not warriors. We will see now if they will do that."

"But —"

Jack lifted a hand and stopped her. "You will speak before all of them."

"What will I say? You have already said no to what the peace men told me to say to you."

"That I and the warriors who follow me come out, too?" Jack said disdainfully.

Winema nodded her round head, her eyes watching him intently. "You must do it, Kientepoos," she pleaded. "The peace men are good men. They do not want to fight again. They think there are many Modoc braves in the rocks who want to surrender but are afraid they would be killed if they tried. The peace men think these would follow you, and that they can protect you with troops while you bring them out."

That verified Jack's suspicion that another major attack was about to be launched. It would be much less bloody for the soldiers if he and some of his warriors could be coaxed out beforehand. Jack turned away from her beseeching eyes. He knew that a great deal of intimidation had been practiced upon the lesser warriors by his opposers. Maybe he himself had misjudged the number who would follow him if they thought they could escape the wrath of the dissidents. Maybe that was the way out of the impasse. Jack shook his head sternly. No, that was the way of disloyalty.

"You will tell the people everything," he said. "Come on."

Winema objected no more and followed him into the open, their emergence magnetizing the warriors and old men, the women and children who awaited them. Escorting Winema, Jack took his place in the circle of headmen, and the rest pressed in closer. They all stood — Curly Doctor, Schonchin John and Hooker Jim together, with their most fanatic supporters flanking them. Scarface Charley had moved into position between them and the chief.

Jack held up his arm, and at his nod Winema repeated the message she had brought from the peace men. It laid a hush on the assemblage, and Jack saw the scowls darken on the countenances of his rivals.

"They want Modocs to fight Modocs!" Schonchin John said furiously. "Then they can come in and kill us!"

Winema looked at him disdainfully. "You are wrong. I say with my heart they only want to stop the war. They do not want to kill old men and women and little children. They do not want to kill warriors who have not murdered white people."

That eliminated all but Hooker Jim and the warriors who had followed him in the massacre of the white ranchers. This fraction felt its conspicuousness and grew restless and uneasyeyed, made uncomfortably aware by Winema that they were asking all to die to prolong their own guilty lives. But Curly Doctor was enamored of the prestige he had enjoyed since the victory over the army. Schonchin John, always jealous of Jack's leadership, saw his chances of gaining it slipping away forever if he did not dominate this crisis.

Stepping into view, Schonchin John pointed an arm and brown finger at the acknowledged chief. In his intensity, he slipped into the jargon English that was nearly as natural to the younger of them as the Modoc tongue. "Jack, you have Winema make speech. How come you no just slip away like yellow dog?"

Jack's body stiffened. Schonchin John was making his play, a moment that had been bound to come. Jack said in the same guttural jargon, "Jack no yellow dog, Schonchin," and a growl of agreement echoed him from the assemblage. "We vote."

A smile broke on Schonchin John's surly lips. "You wantta make deal, Jack? If vote go your way, we all do what you say. If vote go our way, all do what we say. No Modoc fight Modoc. All do same."

Jack's stolid face betrayed no part of what he felt. He had suspected that the peace commission's offer would not be accepted in its presented form. But he had hoped that the issue might lead to the noncombatants' being allowed to leave the stronghold unmolested. Now Schonchin John had flung down the gauntlet. Jack knew that if he declined to pick it up he would have lost face and, with it, most of his influence. If he lost, he would be abdicating to Schonchin

John in everything except nominal leadership, accepting once and for all a fight to the death as the only course open to them, agreeing to any bloody move his opposers might desire. But the people knew that, and if they supported him instead of Schonchin John, he could lead them now to peace.

He said gruffly, "So be it."

Schonchin John walked arrogantly away, moving off to a clear space, stopping and turning to face the people, his head up, arms folded across his chest. The medicine man and Hooker Jim went to him immediately, towing the die-hard clique, while Scarface Charley moved to Jack. The families waited, hushed and motionless. Winema's face had sagged. For a long moment, no one knew what else would happen. Only the fighting men could vote. They seemed hung in uncertainty except for the guilty, who had moved behind Hooker Jim. Then the others followed, moving three out of four to join the proudly watching Schonchin John.

Jack closed his eyes and again said, "So be it."

He knew from the faces of the families that most of them were with him and the warriors who had come to his side. Curtly he told Charley to escort Winema back toward the army post. She said nothing, but her eyes glistened moistly while she turned and followed Scarface. Jack waved for the others to disperse. Even Schonchin John had been impressed by what he read in so many faces. It was all that kept him from pushing for complete leadership on the spot.

But he lingered, Curly Doctor and Hooker Jim with him. When they were alone with Jack, Schonchin said, "You get surprise, Jack?"

Jack grunted. "A little. Not much."

"You keep bargain?"

"I keep bargain."

The trio turned and walked off.

CHAPTER XIII

Little had ever been done to wrest Forbidden Canyon from the wilderness, to which it seemed to have returned completely. Each day, in the four weeks since Wendy had fled from him to vanish into the lava beds, Zack had ridden in, in a thin but persistent hope that she had returned to her old home. This time, like all the others, he found nothing but a deserted cabin which held a table on which lay a combing set. He might as well face the truth. There was nothing to bring her back. Her decision had been final.

Even so, Zack found it impossible to give her up, and once more he fought down the urge to penetrate the lavas himself, with the odds greatly against his getting out alive. He had considered riding up to the army base to ask the peace commissioners to try to get a message to her in the negotiating they were trying to do with the Modocs. But there was nothing with which to convince Wendy that she had been released from her pledge in Dunes' last moment of life.

She knew of no alternative to what she had done except a life in Forbidden Canyon more lonely than before. His friendship, his gift, could not have conveyed his need and desire and abiding love for her. Her last significant encounter with the white race had been at the hands of Monk Sleeper. It could have turned her irrevocably to the Indians, regardless of her promise to her father.

Zack swung into the saddle and rode back down the creek toward the Wagonwheel.

Monk's vicious attack had at least checked the Sleepers for a while as effectively as had the wound from which Purdy was now all but recovered. The sheriff had come out finally, bringing the county coroner. On the way from Yreka he had stopped at ranches and picked up enough men to form a jury so an inquest could be held in the Wagonwheel. There had been no question as to Dunes' murderer and the motive; the sign was still in evidence. Rocked back on their heels, the remaining Sleepers had not made an issue over Monk's death, although they came to the inquest on him. But they resented it. Zack had caught them looking at him with hate-filled eyes. Afterward, with the help of his lake neighbors, Zack had buried Dunes in Forbidden Canyon, where he had spent so much of his unhappy life.

Zack emerged from the Coyote stricture to see a horse and rider passing abreast of him a hundred or so yards out on the basin floor. He had never seen the horse, but the slight figure of the man energized him. Zack went pelting toward him, yelling.

"Hey, you — Ernie!"

The other swung his horse in surprise, then waved an arm over his head. He was Ernie Yost, not only out of the army hospital but sitting a saddle. They rode speedily toward each other, leaned out to shake hands, then settled their horses to a standstill.

"I was swingin' outta my way to Hub Lake to see you," Ernie said. "You saved me a ride."

"Am I glad to see you! How are you?"

Ernie patted his right leg. "Still got her, and even if she ain't as good as she used to be, she still works."

"Did you come by the army camp?" Zack hoped that he had seen Del.

Ernie shook his head. "Only stopped to gas a bit with the detail at the signal station, which was on my way here. Hell's poppin' up there, which is one of the things I had to tell you."

"What now?" Zack frowned, thinking of both Del and Wendy.

"Them Modocs sucked the peace commission into a trap and shot the hell out of it. Canby and the preacher, Thomas, are dead. Meacham's so full of lead they don't give him a show to live. Dyer got away. So did Riddle and Winema; they went along to interpret."

Zack felt as if a pound of buckshot had been dumped in his stomach. The development meant that the last slender hope of a peaceful settlement was gone and that he would be called back to the Rifles. To go in against the stronghold again, this time with Wendy there. He said in an all-gone voice, "Oh no."

"It's God's truth," Ernie said somberly.

After rejecting an offer to permit such of them as wanted to surrender to come out under army protection, Ernie explained, the Modocs had seemed to do an about-face. Two of them, Bogus Charley and Boston Charley, had come to army headquarters. Meacham had been away, but the Indians had talked with Reverend Thomas and told him that the Modocs had had a change of heart. They wanted to talk to the commissioners at a point halfway between the army post and the stronghold where, sometime previously, a tent had been set up for the council that had never come off. They had wanted all the white peace men to come and talk with their own headmen and had asked that they come unarmed to show that their hearts were as good as claimed.

Nearly everyone had smelled a rat except the sky pilot, Ernie said. Thomas had been brimful of faith in God, whom he had credited with the Indians' unexpected about-face, and he had insisted that a show of love was all the Modocs needed now to become meek as lambs. Meacham and Dyer had called it sheer trickery, with which the squaw man, Frank Riddle, and his Modoc wife had agreed heartily. John Fairchild likewise had taken a cynical attitude, as had most of the military who had gone up against Jack's little band in January.

General Canby, however, had leaned Thomas's way. This had not been out of religious fervor, for he had worn two hats: as a member of the peace commission and as the commanding general of the Military Department of the Columbia. Secretary Delano, Department of the Interior, had ordered the commission to council with the Modocs and secure a treaty of peace. William Tecumseh Sherman, Commanding General of the Army, had tartly instructed Canby by telegram, via Yreka, to make peace or war, his department not caring much which it was as long as something was done to end the embarrassing situation.

So Canby had been for meeting the Indians, since the council tent was in sight of the signal station on the bluff and help could be rushed to the scene if anything went wrong. Word had been sent back to the stronghold that the commissioners would come to the tent provided that only an equal number of Indians came, similarly unarmed to show their good faith.

"The signal station kept glasses on that tent every minute," Ernie told Zack, "and pretty soon sent word to headquarters that five Modocs had come to the tent unarmed. What nobody thought of was that the redskins could stash guns and extra Injuns in the rocks the night before — before they put out their invitation. Dyer said the powwow had hardly got started when the Modocs opened up. The ones in the rocks even tossed guns in to the bucks at the powwow. Them that was leery all along made tracks, and the two trustin' souls, Thomas and Canby, got killed." Ernie looked solemn. "I keep wonderin' if Thomas still had his faith in God's help while he was dyin' out there."

"That sure doesn't sound like Captain Jack to me," Zack said with a shake of the head.

"He was there. Winema said they had a vote whether to do things his way or Schonchin John's, and Schonchin won."

Five hundred troops had gone boiling to the scene, Ernie went on, but too late. The Modocs had slipped away into the lava beds. At the same time Curly Doctor and another Modoc had gone in to Captain Mason's camp at the eastern outpost, carrying a flag of truce. They had asked for Mason to come out and talk with them, but the captain had refused. Major Boyle and Lieutenant Sherwood, however, had offered to see what they wanted. No sooner had they got close to the Modocs than they were shot at by a rifle hidden by the white flag. The officers had turned and fled, but Sherwood's thigh had been broken by another shot. It would have been his finish had not the army sentries rushed to the rescue and driven the Modocs back into the lavas.

"They wanted Mason," Ernie said. "Tried to wipe out the whole set of bigwigs in one swoop. What do you think of that?"

"What I've always thought," Zack said. "They're the coolest customers around."

The army, Ernie concluded, had been a hornets' nest, eager to swarm all over the lava beds then and there, but Colonel Gillem had restrained the men. He had been ill and confined to his cot for days and had seemed dazed by the Modocs incredible audacity. He had a company of Indian scouts coming from the Warm Springs reservation. They were good trackers who had served the army in the Paiute war a few years earlier. The scouts had not arrived, and Gillem refused to order his command into the lavas without them. With Canby dead, he was presently the senior officer in the entire Northwest, and that was it. But the army was going in again. There was no doubt of that left.

"I'm sure glad you got home before Fairchild called me back to the Rifles," Zack said. "Hollis Brown'll be gladder yet. The Sleepers'll move now, sure as shootin', the way they did the last time the Modocs tasted blood. They know the fightin'll start up again and I'll be called out of the Wagonwheel for God knows how long."

"That notion's been buzzin' in my head all the way from Tule Lake," Ernie confessed. "It wouldn't be hard to persuade the country that, since the Modocs've kicked up their heels again, they'd massacred every livin' soul in the Wagonwheel."

They separated, Ernie riding on south. Zack turned eastward toward Pistol Peak.

He put in the rest of the day preparing to return to the Rifles, for he knew the call would come at any moment. As the day progressed he grew increasingly troubled. It was bad enough having to help attack the place where Wendy had gone for refuge. A fog would not interfere with military operations a second time and this late in the season, and the Modocs would suffer this time, too. On top of that, the army had brought together a lot of artillery. It would shell the stronghold like no position had ever been shelled, and no distinction could be made between warriors and noncombatants in that kind of assault.

Zack decided to ride over to Ridge Agee's and tell him of the new developments. He fixed and ate a hurried, early supper, then saddled a fresh horse and headed south. He had reached the east end of Hub Lake and was within sight of Agee's buildings when he saw three riders break out of a willow screen ahead. They were coming his way, and he recognized Agee, Trinkler and Ernie Yost. Recognizing him, they hurried. Even as he met them, Zack knew from the deep grimness of their faces that something new had happened.

In a breathless, raging voice, Ernie said, "I got home a trifle too late."

Weakly, Zack said, "Hollis?"

"The Sleepers got him and left the same grisly mess they left at Johnny Minto's." Ernie paused for breath. "He wasn't at the house, but I thought nothin' of it. His cayuse was gone, he didn't expect me to show, and it was the middle of the day. I'd rid a far piece, and my leg was achin', so I fixed some grub, then rested and waited for him to come home."

Along toward midafternoon, Ernie went on,

he had started to get uneasy. It didn't take Hollis that long to do his riding chores unless he ran into something extra. So Ernie had gone looking for him and found his body in Echo Canyon, way up in the Lizards. "Rim shot," he said angrily. "Then the scalpin' and all that. They took his horse and gun to make it look like that's what they wanted. I found some of their tracks. No shoes on the horses. Modoc work, sure as hell — except we know better."

"They decoyed me into the lavas with that kind of horse tracks," Zack told him. "They've stolen some Indian ponies or taken the shoes off some of their own horses. It looks like you were headin' for my place."

"Yeah," Ridge said. "From what I hear, you'll be leavin', and we ain't crazy enough to set like ducks and wait for 'em to pick the rest of us off one at a time. We're goin' to Big S for a showdown, and we could use your help."

"Dunno if that's smart," Zack said with a shake of the head. "Much as I'd like to. By this time they must have their place fortified. Bustin' into their setup might hand 'em the whole Wagonwheel at once."

"What else can we do?" Fred Trinkler demanded.

"It's too late to help Hollis, but his spread's where you've got to make your stand. Don't let 'em take possession. All three of you fort up there. When you go out somewhere, go in a bunch. I'm bound to be called back to the Rifles, and I might as well report tomorrow as wait till they send for me. Reason I suggest it, Ridge, is that I can take Dora to Van Bremer's on my way and get her out of danger."

Ridge nodded and looked at the other two. "He's right, boys. The thing now's to stop Purdy Sleeper. When Zack and Del get home again, we can do somethin' about throwin' 'em off the range they've grabbed already."

"And," Ernie said bitterly, "something about Johnny Minto and what I found up in Echo Canyon."

It was hard for them not to vent their feelings precipitately, but they were reasonable men and accepted Zack's suggestion. They discussed the details; then Zack rode back to Pistol Peak.

Day was just breaking when he returned to Hub Lake the next morning. Dora was ready to leave with him, resigned at last to the necessity of seeking safety from their enemies. She kissed her father wordlessly, and Zack shook hands with Ridge in the same gravely silent manner. Then he and Dora rode out on the roundabout trail Zack would take on his way to report at the army post.

It was only a three-hour ride to the Van Bremer ranch, where there were people enough to ensure Dora's welfare. She was solemn and had little to say until they parted at the ranch. Then, with a worn smile she said quietly, "I know what you're going through. Del told me how you feel about Wendy Dunes. I'll be thinking about you two, as well as Del, the next few days."

"Thanks, Dora."

"And give Del my love and tell him I know he'll come back to me."

Heartily, Zack said, "I sure will."

He knew it was rough on her, too, here apart from things, left to worry about her father in the Wagonwheel and Del in the lava beds. He rode east, toward whatever destiny held in store for him personally.

CHAPTER XIV

The rocket that streaked up from the signal station on the bluff cut a crimson slash in the thin, gray dawn. On its signal the concussion of massed howitzers, two hundred yards from the lake and a thousand from the stronghold, shook the rocky elevation, to which a pack train had carried the guns at tremendous effort in the night. The shock jarred the rusty-red rock under Zack's feet. Under the whistling shells the troops, in a line anchored on the lake and stretched southward for over a mile, went scrambling forward to tackle once more the rocky purgatory that shielded the enemy.

Zack was not with them, for he had reached army headquarters to learn that the Rifles would not be mustered back into service. They were not needed, for this time a thousand regulars, under Green on the west and Mason on the east, would hurl themselves against the handful of Modocs who, so far, had defied and defeated them. Every lesson learned from that crushing day in January was being employed. Food, kegs of water, reserves of ammunition and reserve troops stood ready to be moved to the fighting lines. Aid stations had been set up, mule and hand litters were ready, and so were boats, while the camp hospital was organized to operate around the clock.

"They underdone it the first time," John Fairchild told Zack, "and this time they may be overdoing it, but I don't think so."

Neither did Zack, who, seeing the onset of this smooth, carefully prepared operation, appreciated Gillem's wisdom in not going off half-cocked after the murder of the peace commissioners four days before.

Zack had been about to return to the Wagon-wheel, and the ranchers he had left there in serious jeopardy, when he found himself called upon to serve in a way he had not anticipated. The civilian packers at the base camp, with other members of the Rifles who had reported for duty, had been summoned to the field hospital by the regimental surgeon. His, Dr. Canabiss had explained, was the only department still seriously short of help. He would need his trained orderlies to assist him, once the fighting started, and could ill spare them for litter bearers.

He had asked for volunteers, and Zack had been among those who had stepped forward, his duty to those at home outweighed momentarily by this horribly necessary service. He stood now at an aid station just south of the elevation where the artillery had been set up. The mounting light was free of fog, and he could see the line of blue-coats moving into the distant rocks. Somewhere far beyond them the screaming shells were falling.

Out on the line Del kept his squads moving

flush with those of the other platoon sergeant. They had already got into the razor-edged rocks and something new — wild gooseberry brush with slashing thorns. Now and then he muttered, "Steady, boys. Long ways to go yet. Damn it, Elva; hold back. The Injuns won't run away before you get your chance to kill a few."

His chiding covered a good deal of feeling for his men, for he knew from a briefing that his company was on the toughest, and what probably would be the bloodiest, sector of the line. Reconnaissance in the idle months had unlocked a few of the lavas' mysteries. Due west of the stronghold, and east of his part of the line, was a flat as nearly level as rock surface could be and some six hundred yards across. The Modocs had outposts all along the outside of the flat, excellently buttressed, while there was no cover at all for assault forces. It was this flat that had ruined the January attack, and it had to be stormed and taken to open the way to the stronghold.

"You're too hungry for Modocs again, Elva."

The line moved unopposed for a long while under cover of the hammering artillery, crawling, climbing, sprawling, bleeding from rock cuts and torn slashes. Far ahead of it shells were bursting, but there was no telling to what effect. The men gained confidence, for as the light grew strong there was promise of weather as fair as it had been lousy the time before. Maybe the big guns had cowed the Modocs, robbed them of their incredible daring. But wait. Somewhere down the line a bugle insinuated into the heavy rumble of artillery the high, sharp call to charge.

"All right, Elva! You can cut loose your wolf!"

Nobody knew what had happened, but Del took his squads forward with the rest of the line in an upright run. For further moments the only firing was that of the distant howitzers and distant explosions somewhere forward. The charge was ragged, with men tripping, to rise with bleeding elbows or knees and catch up. And then came the dreaded sound, a crash of rifles and muskets which was borne in a hail of bullets that swept the ranks. Men folded and went down on either side of Del, and even without fog there was nothing to be seen forward but rock and sagebrush and wisps of rising smoke.

The order to return fire was needless, for new Springfields and aging muskets leaped to blue shoulders and kicked by reflex. The roar swept all along the line, and the battle reached full consummation in the space of a moment. The army firing damped that of the Indians; then once more the Modocs fanned a searing flame over the line. Some of the troops dived for shelter, others fell, threshed or laid still, while the voices of officers and noncoms urged them onward. The bluecoats tried, but in a moment wounded were falling across wounded.

"Fall back!"

It was that or be cut to pieces, but the men remembered what had happened to the dead and wounded previously. This time they doubled the danger to themselves by taking time to support or drag the casualties with them — back to the last ridge they had crossed, where they dug in behind natural fortifications or built new ones out of loose rock.

"Litter bearer — !"

Del realized that they had pulled out of range of the Indians and could not fight from these positions, but the respite was needed. Gaps yawned in the line, and the troops were rattled and disorganized. He looked behind the ridge to see mule litters hurrying in. For a moment he saw Zack, reminding him of the message his brother had brought to him from Dora. He knew he had it better than his brother did. His girl was safely away from this mad hell. Zack's was somewhere deeper in it.

The first shells from the big army guns had fallen short or passed over or landed north or south of the stronghold proper, sending up geysers of rock splinters, the explosions hammering the very air. But the Indians centered quickly until a shell landed squarely on the stronghold floor, hurting no one but filling the whole area with ear-hurting sound and choking dust. The chief had ordered the oldlings and children into the depths of the caves; the younger women and older boys had been assigned to carry ammunition and water. Some of these were knocked down by the concussion, and more shells fell into the stronghold behind the first.

Wendy, loaded down with bladders of water, was moving along a trench that was cut deep in the flat west of the stronghold when rifle fire added its terror to that of the big guns. She ducked down instinctively, only to realize that the rifle fighting was still some distance ahead of her. She listened to the new crash of guns and, in spite of herself, began to shake. She had heard it said that there were twenty soldiers to each Modoc warrior. Brave as they were, she did not see how they could endure very long against such force.

She went resolutely on with her job, the weight of fear adding greatly to her burden. The sound of shooting grew so loud it tickled and hurt her eardrums. Presently she came to a small gully directly behind the Modoc outposts. Queen Mary and some other older women were there at a cache of ammunition, which they would distribute to the line when called for. Nothing about Captain Jack's sister discredited, even now, the name the white people had given her. She stood proudly, betraying no sign of the fear that churned in Wendy's stomach.

Mary glanced at the younger woman and said, "Leave the skins and go back."

Wendy looked at her gratefully. She had expected to have to distribute the water to the warriors. She sensed from something in Mary's expression that she should have done so but was being spared. Wendy put down the water.

"Thank you."

"You should not have stayed with us, little one," Mary said suddenly, her voice kind. "You should have gone back to your people after they did that awful thing to Kientepoos."

"You are my people," Wendy said.

Mary smiled sadly, then turned back to stare at the sound of the fighting, seeming to ignore her completely.

Wendy hurried back along the trench toward the stronghold. There, not long before, she had come upon a second disillusionment, which again had shaken her faith in people. Hooker Jim had been the chief of the people from whom her father had taken a woman to replace her dead mother. Wendy had always looked upon him as being like her father in natural goodness. Yet she had seen him help Curly Doctor and Schonchin John — who to her were repulsive, ill-natured old men — trick Jack and force him to help in the plot to murder the peace men. They had made Jack share their guilt, thus making sure he could never make peace for the sake of those who wanted and truly deserved it. To protect themselves, the unholy trio had consigned everyone to this hell.

That development had filled Wendy again with the revulsion she had felt when Monk Sleeper forced her to go with him to the cave on Juniper Flat. Zack had delivered her from

Monk's hands, yet the sickness in her heart had turned her against him, too, because he was another white man. So she had taken the Big S horse and set forth at once to carry out her father's instructions in case of his death. She had been so completely sure, then, that her father had been right in what he had said about white people's being all the same at heart. Now she knew that there were rotten men even among the Indians.

Wendy halted and turned, realizing that the rifle fire behind her had died down. The tight band around her chest loosened a little. The attack had been beaten off. If only the big guns would stop firing.

As the battle continued, identities were lost as the military machine hurled itself time and again against the tiny force fighting with the fury of cornered animals. Signal flags and heliographs kept the eastern and western assault forces informed of each other's situation. Mason, on the east flank, was forced to check his line until Green's, on the west, could get up over the obstinate flat. The Warm Springs scouts, under half-breed Donald McKay, had joined Mason and were out in front.

While Mason marked time, Green threw his men again and again at the flat. Each time the Modoc outposts threw them back, adding to the casualties that filtered out of the rocks on mule litters or came in to the field hospital from the east side by boat. Finally the artillery tried to shell the obstructing outposts but could not get the range, and since this required lobbing explosives perilously close to Green's line, it was given up. The central and southern part of the western front could not gain a foot. But toward the end of the day the north end made a little headway along the margin of the lake.

This time the attack was to be pressed day and night, giving the Indians no chance to rest. Reinforcements were sent in, and as many of the bone-weary troops as could be spared were brought back to rest. Nearly to the man, the ones who came out were walking wounded, slashed and bleeding from the rocks and the ferocious thorns of the gooseberry brush, if not from bullets. Their replacements dug in on the line, while the howitzers went back to pounding the Indian stronghold. The rifle fire was not as heavy after nightfall, but it kept up, and the night grew cold, and mosquitoes swarmed in from the lake. Back at the field hospital the surgeon and his aides worked through the night. More men were buried in the plot under the bluff that had received its first dead four months before. Many more lay gravely hurt in the tents.

Dawn brought a renewal of the attack with everything the army could muster. The troops had charged over the same ground only to be driven back so many times that they seemed to be caught in an insane seesaw that would go on forever. The howitzers kept lobbing shells into a stronghold that could have no life left in it, but that drew off none of the bitter resistance ahead of the lines. As the day advanced, Green decided to concentrate everything on the essential business of taking the impeding flat. Eagan's company was ordered to make the try while the howitzers again lobbed shells into the Modoc outposts. Eagan's company went boiling forward to be shot to pieces, Eagan falling with it. Spirits fell to zero, then, only to go soaring upward again: in the last two hours of daylight, the Modocs broke on the northern front enough to let the east and west flanks drive in along the lake and join forces.

With that the Modocs were cut off from water, one of the prime objectives. Serious inroads had been made in their ammunition as well, and they had not been permitted even such rest as the troops had gained. The command took heart, only to spend the night fighting back attempt after attempt by the Indians to reopen their access to the lake. At dawn the Modocs gave up the effort, and the litter bearers and ambulance boats shuttled back and forth, taking out a new batch of casualties.

A newspaper correspondent, that morning, rushed to Yreka a dispatch stating that the Modocs had been surrounded and could not escape. But before that got into print, Hooker Jim reminded the command that the south side of the lava beds was still wide open. Leading a band of braves, Hooker crept in on the base camp itself, which was nearly deserted with the command in the lava beds. Hooker was after ammunition and was nearly inside the camp before he was discovered.

All available civilians and the more able of the wounded were armed hastily. The signal station flashed a message to Green that the camp itself was being attacked, and even before this was accomplished Hooker's Indians threw a volley of lead into the tents. For long moments it appeared that the base would be overrun, pouring the dregs of humiliation down the army's throat; then some of the reserves came pounding in from the field. Hooker faded into the rocks empty-handed, but his sally proved that the Modocs had grown desperately short of powder and lead.

The time had come to break their backs, and it was attempted. All through the third night howitzer shells thunked into the Modoc positions to make sure the warriors got no rest. Troops on the line shot at everything that attracted their attention. There was almost no firing from the Indians. Either fatigue was at last overcoming them or their ammunition had run out.

At dawn came the ringing of bugles, ordering a charge.

That time the line swept onto the flat without resistance, went stumbling over the sharp rocks, into and out of crevices. The stubborn outposts were quickly overrun. The troops feared a trap, for nothing on the record could account for such passivity. The south ends of the east and west lines came together in the long-awaited union. Then at last the troops were on the edge of the vaunted stronghold itself, looking down into torn and dusty emptiness.

CHAPTER XV

The emigrant road that passed Tule Lake had, in its two decades of use, developed a substantial reverse traffic between the country along the Oregon-California border and the railroad in Nevada. Leaving the Tule basin, the later wayfarers went up through Fandango Pass and down across Surprise Valley and over the sterile vastness of the Black Rock desert to arrive in the great bend of the Humboldt. In the curve of the great bend, among desert mountains, lay the dwindling Buena Vista mining district. And in this district, ghosting away, was Star City.

Moribund though it was, Star City was not without population or even industry. Its location made it handy to numerous Nevada mining camps that still produced treasure. It was almost on the Central Pacific, over which the treasure was shipped and whose trains had begun to be subject to holdups. Because the camp had retained a few of its saloons, hotels, eating houses, gaming joints and brothels, it had become a favorite hangout for the outlaw population of western Nevada.

Purdy Sleeper, when he arrived in Star City late on a mid-April evening, knew where to find the kind of men he wanted. Within an hour after his arrival he was seated at a table in the Little

Nemo Saloon, hunched over whisky with Big Red Harris, a giant of a man with hair the color of iron rust and a full beard of the same hue. Harris and four intimates had recently been tried and let off for lack of evidence, down in Storey County, in connection with the involuntary stop of a Central Pacific train and the dynamiting of its express car.

"I'm tellin' you, Red," Purdy was saying. "I've got hold of the biggest thing you ever laid eyes on. I'd've had it in my pocket by now, but the bastards organized. So I need help. I guess you heard the latest in that Injun war up there."

Harris eyed him in suspicious interest, used to Purdy's big ideas but aware that sometimes they bore fruit. By then there was no backwash in the country that hadn't heard how Captain Jack had thumbed his nose at the army again, quitting the lava beds and, apparently, vanishing into thin air. The army hadn't seen hide nor hair of his band since the battle.

"I heard," Harris said. "What do you figure to make of it?"

"Plenty," Purdy said in rising excitement. "Mebbe the army don't know where to find old Jack, but me and the boys do. We smelled 'em out, and them Modocs couldn't've suited me better than the place they picked to hole up again. Jack never moved out of the lavas like the army thinks. He just moved to the south edge and right on top of the Wagonwheel."

"Instead of puttin' the world in your pocket,"

Harris said, "it appears to me like you stand to lose your hair."

"That's just the point," Purdy agreed. "Jack don't figure to stay there long. He couldn't. I think he's getting set to run, and a likely place to pick up supplies and maybe some ammunition is in the Wagonwheel."

"So you pull off that raid and lay it to them, gettin' rid of those fellas you say have bunched up against you. There's three of you Sleepers. Why do you want me and the boys?"

"We gotta make sure. A way to do it's to pull off a raid so big we couldn't possibly be accused of it."

"It'd sure look funny," Harris rejoined, "if you Sleepers come through a raid like that without a scratch."

Purdy grinned. "Us Sleepers'll take care of ourselves."

"You usually do," Harris agreed. He ruminated for a long moment, nodding his shaggy head. "What'd there be in it for me and the boys except the risk?"

"Them lava beds," Purdy said readily. "You help me get a grip on Tule basin, and you're set. You can have you a gang as big as old Jack's. With me runnin' the country outside, ready to tip you off, you could stand off a whole army of lawmen."

Harris combed his fingers through his heavy beard. "By damn," he mused.

"That big enough, Red?" Purdy murmured.

Harris didn't have to answer, for Purdy knew he was thinking of the scores of rich mining camps within easy striking distance of the stronghold, of the outlaw force he could gather there, larger by far than the fifty-sixty Modocs who had stood off so big an army. He was thinking of a veritable outlaw kingdom that he would rule.

Purdy, when he conceived it, had found the idea just as attractive to himself. There were no lengths to which he could not go with Harris and a huge gang of outlaws right there to back him up.

Harris leaned forward eagerly. "I always took you for a kind of blowhard, Purdy. I apologize."

When Purdy left the Little Nemo he was completely satisfied. Three days later he was back on Big S.

The Sleepers sat up late that night, talking while they worked on a jug of whisky Purdy had brought home from Nevada. The session was not without its tensions. Rip, during his father's absence, had been up to Tule Lake to check on the army's latest intentions, which seemed to be thoroughly unsettled.

The three-day battle had produced few results beyond a staggering number of new casualties. The several newspaper correspondents who had been on hand had reported the hollow victory to a nation already highly critical. The citizenry closer at hand was up in arms about it. Colonel Gillem was coming in for the same tongue-lashing Wheaton had suffered. The vaunted Warm Springs scouts had occupied the stronghold and, after halfhearted attempts to track the Modocs, reported that they seemed to have fled toward Pit River.

"We know better than that," Purdy scoffed. "Them Warm Springs don't hanker to get their tail feathers shot off, that's all."

"I don't blame 'em," Rip said worriedly. "When I looked at the size of that army outfit and seen how much of it wound up in the hospital or under the ground —" He lifted his hands helplessly. "Well, I got a funny feelin' about them Modocs being right on top of the Wagonwheel. They *could* clean out the Wagonwheel, us included."

Frank laughed. "If we're found scalped and butchered, Rip, nobody's gonna blame us any more for what happened to Johnny Minto and old Hollis Brown."

Rip scowled. While Monk was alive, he had been the butt of their ridicule, including Rip's own. Now Monk was gone, making Rip the youngest and therefore the natural target. He said, "There's somethin' else. The Rifles wasn't called up again. Zack Buckman's back here."

That brought a glittering hardness to Purdy's eyes. Whether or not they had felt affection for Monk, he had been a Sleeper and Buckman had killed him. That had set up a blood feud that all three of them acknowledged. Purdy said, "The son of a bitch. He hole up with the other three at Brown's place?"

Frank shook his head. "They're holed up, but they moved over to Pistol Peak. Got Buckman's place fortified like a stockade. I took a look with glasses. They'd sure of had us stood off if you hadn't made a deal with Red Harris."

"They sure would've," Purdy agreed. "But I made a deal. You locate us some more Injun ponies? Red said to get him a dozen."

"I spotted ponies," Frank said. "There's some Pit Rivers camped at Medicine Lake. Twenty or so lodges. Their ponies're up the creek from the camp. Easy to pick off."

"We'll get 'em tomorrow night."

Rip looked up from a moody study of the tabletop. "When you gonna pull it off?"

"Pull what off?" Purdy said innocently.

"That fake massacre. Damn it, you know what I mean."

"It won't be fake. It's gonna be real."

"All right, but when?"

"Not," Purdy said, "till them Modocs get restless and start prowlin' around. It's got to look good this time. If we work it right, it'll look real good."

"When's Red gonna show?" Frank asked.

"He ain't showin' here. I'm meetin' him in the Moccasins day after tomorrow night."

The next night the three Sleepers slipped in on the pony band of the indolent Pit River Indians camped at Medicine Lake. So skilled had they grown at such involuntary changes of ownership that they had cut out the animals they needed and hazed them some distance northward before the inevitable dogs at the village grew uneasy and announced their suspicions to the night. The Pits were as aware as the Sleepers that their ancient enemies, the Modocs, were only a few miles north of them. As Purdy had predicted, they seemed to attribute the raid to them and did not come boiling out to defend their property. The ponies were driven speedily along the ridges of the Lizards and left penned in a box canyon in the Moccasins.

"So this is where Harris'll hole up," Rip commented.

Purdy delighted in being secretive. It seemed to enhance his feeling of importance. He only grunted.

The next night, however, the Sleepers met Harris outside the Moccasins and guided him to the box canyon. Harris brought eight men he had persuaded to join him in the venture and the life of lawless freedom that was to follow it. They were a hard-bitten lot that even the Sleeper sons eyed with respect. They brought several packhorses loaded with camp supplies, enough to sustain them in the backlands for quite a while.

At dawn Purdy stood with Harris on a knob that gave them a good view of the Wagonwheel, with which the red-bearded man was unfamiliar. While Harris examined the detail through field glasses, Purdy explained matters.

"You and your boys," he said, as calmly as if they were planning the spring's calf roundup, "will light the fuse at Big S. Shoot up the buildings and burn my barn."

Harris swung his head to look at him. "What's the matter? Don't you need a barn?"

"I can afford a new one. And it'll let us out if somebody comes around with questions."

"Then what?" Harris asked.

"Me and the boys'll beat off the attack. Don't worry; everybody'll shoot high. Then we'll join you and get in on the fun. We'll come along the south side of the lake. Burn the Minto buildings, even if there ain't anyone living there now. It's got to look good. The same at old Hollis Brown's place, over there to the left. So on till we hit Pistol Peak, over there to the north. There's where we'll get a fight. It's Zack Buckman's spread. He showed up while I was in Nevada, and they're all ganged at his place. Four of 'em now."

"Just waitin' for you to come and get 'em?"

Purdy shook his head. "They're out and around days, but always in a bunch."

Harris said with assurance, "All you gotta do is say when."

Purdy nodded. "Just keep your outfit outta sight till I do."

The Sleepers headed back to Big S through the Lizard foothills. They were riding in toward headquarters, in midmorning, when Rip, with his superior eyesight, raised on the stirrups and

189

stared forward for a moment.

"Horsebackers at our place," he reported. "Quite a bunch. Damn me if they don't look like army."

"What the hell?" Frank muttered.

"We'll see, by God." Purdy spurred belligerently forward.

There were two squads of mounted troopers waiting in the space between the house and the barn. They apparently had just arrived, for none of them had dismounted. The sergeant in charge was Del Buckman.

"What're you doin' here?" Purdy demanded.

Del's eyes were cloudy with matters Purdy knew had little to do with army affairs. He said curtly, "Stopped by with a tip. Seen you coming and waited. You could have Indians on top of you any time." He nodded toward the Coyotes. "They're just on the far side of those hills."

Purdy realized that the army had located Jack finally. That was fine. They'd stir the Modocs up, which was all Purdy was waiting for. He grinned jeeringly. "You lunkheads just find that out? We knew it days ago."

"It was my duty to warn you, Sleeper," Del said coldly. "Not my pleasure."

He started to swing his horse, but Rip said uneasily, "Wait a minute. They been up to something new?"

"That's what I might've told your father if he'd had the sense to be worried. They've smelled blood again. Now that they've been located, they won't stay where they are. They'll either move your way or east."

"Smelled blood?" Purdy said. "Where?"

"Black Ledge. They ambushed a patrol. Seventy-six men, Sleeper, and fifty-three were either killed or wounded. But you figure to do better, I guess, if they land on top of you."

He spoke a command, and the detachment rode out, heading east down the north side of the Wagonwheel. Purdy knew they were going to Pistol Peak, probably to give the same warning. If Zack and the others took it and left till the Modocs were driven out of the vicinity, the whole plan was ruined.

"Criminy," Rip said in a hollow voice. "That's the biggest bloodletting yet. We're crowdin' our luck to hang around here."

"Only if that bunch at Pistol Peak rabbits on us," Purdy said coolly. "If they don't, our luck's never been as sweet. Didn't Del Buckman himself spread the warning that the Wagonwheel stood to be raided?"

But his relish in the day, his sureness of his ability to gain everything he wanted were suddenly roiled and diminished. He wondered if there had been any massacre at Black Ledge. Del knew what was really happening in the Wagonwheel as well as Zack did. Maybe they were trying to set a trap of their own.

"You boys get to work," he said waspishly. "I'm going up on Sentinel Peak with the glasses and keep an eye on that army bunch."

The lofty stone pillar not far from his headquarters figured in his plan with Harris, for he was to send up a smoke from it on the day he wanted Harris to take action. But half an hour later he was there for a wholly unexpected reason. His glasses picked up the army detachment, which was riding down the valley at a trot. He swung the glasses toward the far Moccasins in a sudden worry that there might be smoke coming up from Harris's camp. He saw none.

He waited with hunched shoulders in a patient vigil until the detail vanished into the timber along Pistol Creek. He could see nothing beyond. Within half an hour it reappeared and, to his surprise, headed south. It dawned on him that they were going into the Pit River country, where there were numerous settlers, with their warning. They were very apt to discover the Indian village at Medicine Lake and learn of the ponies apparently stolen by the Modocs. If the troopers set out to track those ponies! He watched, fighting his jumpy nerves, until the detail vanished into the far Lizards.

CHAPTER XVI

Ernie Yost was first to see the army detachment riding in. All four of the men presently staying at Pistol Peak had been up in Forbidden Canyon that morning, for Zack still checked daily in the dying hope that Wendy had at last returned. It was getting on toward noon when they got back, and while they were branding calves as best they could under the circumstances they had decided to eat before riding out again. Ernie was on the porch, for one of them was always on the lookout. He yelled into the house, where Zack and the other two were rustling grub.

"Hey, Zack! Bet you can't guess who's comin' to pay a call!"

Zack came to the door just as Del's detail rode in. He knew that this was anything but a casual visit squeezed into Del's duties. But they had all greeted each other with pleasure before Del told them what had happened at Black Ledge, which was hardly more than a skip and a jump from the Wagonwheel.

The Warm Springs scouts on whom Colonel Gillem had depended to track down the Modoc renegades had done anything but a wholehearted job. But the signal station on top of the bluff above the army camp had kept a constant watch over the lava beds with telescopes. For days they had seen nothing to indicate where Captain Jack might have re-established himself, if he was still in the lavas rather than decamped, as the Warm Springs trackers suggested.

Then, maybe through carelessness on the part of the Modocs or, as Del now suspected, for bait, a very definite smoke had been spotted. It had seemed to be in the heart of the lavas and some five or six miles from the old stronghold. Gillem, his fingers stinging from his experience in the lavas only nine days before, had ordered a scout in force. Captain Thomas had been given command, and his sixty-six regulars, five officers, a surgeon, three packers and a civilian guide had been sent forth with orders to go as far south as Black Ledge. They were to determine the exact Modoc position and find another, if possible, from which it could be shelled. Under no circumstances were they to provoke an attack by the Modocs. Fourteen of the Warm Springs scouts had been ordered out of the stronghold, which they still occupied, to meet Thomas somewhere down the line.

The patrol had struck out at daybreak, the men heartened by the chance for another crack at the Modocs in spite of the colonel's orders to avoid contact. Once the detachment had got down in the country it was to explore, however, it had lost some of its sense of well-being. The area had been extremely rough, the solid slag sea of the beds to the north giving way to small, interlocking basins and gullies; snaking, rocky defiles; traverse dikes and plateaus — any part of which would serve the Modocs handsomely if they had chosen to set up an ambush. But the patrol had scrambled, slid and stumbled on, waiting for contact with the Warm Springs scouts, who had failed to put in an appearance. Sometime before noon the command had come to a dike of broken lava, lying upon more ancient rock, that lay squarely across the route. This had been Black Ledge, the terminus of the scout. But the orders had been to proceed to the southern end of the dike, which would require five more miles of arduous going.

The country at the southern end of the ledge had been the worst yet. Deeply channeled and raggedly rimmed, it had been a fair replica of the stronghold to the north, although there had been no sign of the Modocs' having used it. Thomas had ordered a noon halt, and the detail had occupied the rugged site, hungry and worn down. They had stacked their rifles, and some of them had tugged the boots off their hot, blistered feet. All of them, when they had eaten their rations, had searched their clothing and bodies for the perniciously boring wood ticks of the region.

After a rest, Lieutenant Cranston, who had not liked the look of things, had asked and received permission to scout over a ridge to the southeast. With twelve volunteers he had struck out, and he had barely disappeared over the ridge when the percussion of many more guns than Cranston carried had rolled back to the main command. Even as the men had sprung to their feet a volley of shots had swept through them, too, coming from the rocks all around them.

The troops had gone scuttling into the nearest cover, some without boots and guns. Thomas, nearly as panicked as the men, had tried to hold them in some sort of order and move them into a defensive position on the sidehill opposite the main attack. The Modocs had shot this effort to pieces, killing Lieutenant Harrison, then Thomas himself, then Lieutenant Wright. After that the rocky depression had been a slaughter pen in which three-fourths of the command had died or been wounded gravely. The rest had simply crawled off into the rocks and hidden. Then the Modocs, satisfied with the results, had pulled out.

Only then had the Warm Springs scouts put in an appearance, and they at least had served to carry word of the disaster to Gillem at the base camp. The horrified colonel had ordered every available man into the field, but before the relief expedition could reach the scene of the massacre night had fallen and pinned it down where it was until morning.

Del had been with the second column, and he concluded, "You can't imagine a more sickenin' sight. Cranston's patrol was wiped out to the man. Bodies all over the place where the main command was hit. The wounded laid there on the rocks all that afternoon and night, thirsty and then cold, expecting every minute for the Modocs to come back for their scalps. It took the next day and night to get 'em in to the base. Couldn't use mule litter. It took six men to the stretcher. There was a whole pack train of mules, though. Loaded with dead men."

"Rough," Zack said, shaking his head. "And stupid."

"It was both," Del agreed.

But there was no mystery now about the Modocs' whereabouts, which was somewhere between Black Ledge and Sandy Bluff. Meanwhile, General Jeff C. Davis, replacement of the murdered Canby, had arrived at the base camp. After he had taken personal command, his first move had been to order the base transferred out of the lavas and to John Fairchild's ranch, where the situation was much more comfortable. This was presently being done, while two companies of cavalry, one of artillery, and the Warm Springs scouts patrolled the southern edge of the lavas, hoping to cut off Jack's escape. Since this was no guarantee against escape, Del's patrol had been sent to warn such settlers as might find themselves in the path of the Modocs.

Del went on with his detail, saying he would be back through the next day. For a moment afterward, the four men left behind regarded each other. "Well," Trinkler reflected, "old Purdy couldn't ask for a better setup than he's got now."

That expressed what they all were feeling.

They ate their noon meal, then rode over to Agee's north range to continue with the calf branding they were conducting on a piecemeal basis as they could. The evenings were growing long, with May nearly arrived, so they worked late. By the time they had eaten supper, dusk hovered over the Wagonwheel.

Nights for a long while had been the time of greatest tension. Zack's reason for asking the others to move to his place was the fact that from Pistol Peak the entire Wagonwheel could usually be seen in the moonlight and starlight that prevailed at that season. Trinkler rode up the slope to the lookout point right after supper, and when Zack relieved him a few hours later, Trinkler seemed worried.

"Maybe my eyes tricked me, Zack," he confided. "But when I first come up here, damned if I didn't get the idea I seen smoke liftin' off Sentinel Peak. Sort of dyin' away, like it had been goin' big earlier, when there was more light. By the time I noticed it, it was so dark I wasn't sure I seen anything at all."

"Smoke?" Zack said. "Like Indian signals?"

"Well, I sure don't know why anybody'd build a campfire up there," Trinkler said doggedly. "Shouldn't've said anything, maybe. But it kind of boogered me."

Zack looked off toward Sentinel, far up the basin and not a great way from Big S headquarters. "Don't see any reason for a signal either," he commented. "Unless Purdy's in cahoots with the Modocs. I doubt that."

"Reckon I was seein' spooks," Trinkler said, and walked off down the slope toward the house.

Zack tried to dismiss it, but, as had been the case with Trinkler, it stuck in his mind. The night was clear again, and he found himself looking time after time in the direction of Sentinel Peak. Yet he had more than the Wagonwheel to watch as a source of trouble now. There were the passes through which Modocs would ride if they came into the basin for supplies. Pistol Pass was easy to keep an eye on, but the other that they could use — between the Coyote and Wildhorse hills — was too distant.

It was nearly the end of his watch when his shifting gaze settled suddenly on the far hills, on past Sentinel Peak. After lifting the glasses, he got the focus and drew sure of a dab of red over there at the foot of those hills. He stood frozen, watching the light grow brighter and become a glow. Fire, and at Big S itself. The distance was too great for him to hear shooting, if such there had been. But if the Sleepers were catching it, it was an Indian raid. They would have come through that pass down there.

This was something much different from what he had expected to face.

He went rushing down to the house, roused the others and told them what was happening. "No telling how many there are," he concluded, "or how far they mean to go. But we've got to get set for the worst."

"If they'd knock off the Sleepers and quit," Ernie commented, dressing hurriedly, "I'd ride up there and shake their hands."

Ten minutes later, with all of them on the peak, they knew it was a full-scale raid. Fire had broken out over at the old Minto place, pretty definitely making it Indians. "Lootin'," Ridge said, "and burnin' what they can't use. Boys, I worked hard for my place. I can't set up here and watch 'em burn me out."

"We can't stop what the army can't," Zack reminded him. "We'd only throw away our lives if we tried."

When presently they realized that the Brown buildings were burning on the far side of Hub Lake, there was no doubt that it was to be a clean sweep of the Wagonwheel. They still had spotted no riders, for the raiders could not have chosen a better route to keep themselves concealed from anyone who might be looking from Pistol Peak. At first there had been the masking background of the dark, far hills. Now the lake timber intervened.

"They're on their way here," Ernie said finally. "Which do we do — fight or hide?"

"Zack's right," Ridge reflected. "We can't stand off the kind of war party that would dare do this. I say hide. Think up here's all right, Zack? Would they come lookin' for us?"

"Not if they're Modocs," Zack said. "They

wouldn't know we're here." He looked suddenly at Trinkler. "What about that smoke you thought you seen on Sentinel Peak? By damn, you did see a smoke. Somethin' is fishy about this." He lifted a hand and rubbed his jaw. "You suppose Purdy recruited help from somewhere and that smoke was the go-ahead signal?"

"If you're right," Ridge said bitterly, "he'll sure know we're here. Where do you think we ought to go, Zack'"

Promptly, Zack said, "Forbidden Canyon. It used to strike me that Dunes could've stood off a fair-sized army there. Only way in is up or down the crick. Let's grab some grub and what ammunition we can carry and get over there."

The others were in wholehearted agreement, for it was a wise move no matter who they faced. It meant the sacrifice of their buildings, but no doubt remained that they would need luck to get off with their lives. They worked swiftly, and half an hour later, with evidence, above the far lake growth, that Trinkler's buildings had been put to the torch, they rode northwest toward the foot of the Coyote Hills.

An hour later Zack found himself flattened on the rim on the east side of Coyote Creek, at the edge of the basin. Ernie was stationed across the creek from him, while Ridge and Trinkler had gone up the creek to guard that entrance to the hidden canyon. They all had rifles and enough ammunition to hold out longer than any raider, white or red, would dare to press an attack. The night had grown cold, but Zack hardly noticed that, although he lay motionless, his eyes squinted as much from anger as from his intent sweeping of the far night with his field glasses. His own place was much nearer at hand than the others had been while they had looked on from Pistol Peak.

The conflagration at Big S had nearly died out, suggesting that it had not been a big one to begin with. But now Ridge's buildings, on the east end of the lake, were burning furiously. Pistol Peak would be next, and Zack's glasses carefully swept the distance between the two places. It was not long until, far over there and almost too minute and benighted to detect, a party came moving across the bottom. Its members were bunched and rode swiftly, knowing exactly where they were going. But at first he could tell nothing at all about them.

What was revealed came through their actions while they approached Pistol Peak. Even Modocs would have to allow for there being someone on hand to contest them, but this bunch rode in with a special wariness. They spread out to circle the buildings, then dismounted, moved in on foot, and then were lost from sight. A moment later the very faint sound of shooting came through the night: test shots to see if the place was occupied or to draw fire and join a fight. This occupied only a moment's time; then silence returned to the darkness.

Zack spent a long while in the agony of waiting to see his own buildings, erected at so much hard labor, give way to the torch. But it didn't happen, which convinced him that those were not Modocs, who would have spared nothing in the Wagonwheel. Yet the riders did not reappear, and he guessed that they were conducting a search for victims they expected but would not find, proof positive that they were well acquainted in the Wagonwheel.

The silence continued another long while, and then he saw the riders back at their horses, swinging up in a way that suggested they were riding bareback. This did not deceive him, for, instead of going on toward Pistol Pass to quit the basin, they rode south again, this time angling off toward the Moccasin Hills. He followed them with the glasses until, all at once, they vanished from sight over there. He knew they had gone into the hills.

Five minutes later he met Ernie on the creek bank. "What do you make of that?" Ernie said bitterly.

"I'm sure of one thing," Zack said. "Purdy used up his fake Indian raid on nothing at all. I bet he's fit to be tied."

"That's gotta be it," Ernie agreed. "He's come by a wolf pack somehow, and it's a good thing we decided to lay low. And here. They beat the hell outta Pistol Peak tryin' to find us. Didn't even burn you out. No use, when all that big buildup come to nothin'."

"His help's holed up in the Moccasins," Zack

reflected. "Ridge knows those hills like his own hand. He'll have an idea where the hide-out is."

"We gonna jump it?"

"Not by ourselves. But Del's comin' back through here tomorrow." Zack rubbed a hand over his tired eyes. "Meanwhile we might as well go home and get some rest. Purdy's got to think up a new one before he moves again."

CHAPTER XVII

The cavalry detachment came out of the Lizards at a point that let it see below it the smoking ruins of both Trinkler's and Agee's ranch buildings. A trooper breathed, "Jesus, they've been here!" And Del Buckman took his outfit down the grade at a gallop. He knew the occupants of the burned houses had banded together at Pistol Peak, and he lost no time getting over the bottom to see what had happened there. When he led his detail into an intact ranch headquarters and saw four able-bodied men waiting for him, he pushed back his hat and scratched his head.

"You fellas got a pull with old Jack?" he said as he swung out of the saddle.

Zack told him what had happened, and of the white renegades they believed to be holed up in the Moccasins. Del listened with a darkening countenance, then, in conclusion, shook his head.

"You boys must've been mistaken. That was Modoc work."

Zack's eyes widened. "Even if they hadn't gone the wrong way leaving here," he retorted, "the fact that they didn't burn this place proves who they were. Right now Purdy's cussing himself for burning the others, when he figures he can make use of 'em pretty soon."

"Can't agree it was Sleeper," Del said stubbornly. "And a good thing. I've got no authority to do law work against white men. Modocs is somethin' else, and this sure looks like Modoc work to me." He shifted his gaze to his grinning men. "Don't it to you, boys?" he asked them.

"Sure does," a lanky corporal answered. "And if they're holed up around here, it's our job to pay 'em a visit."

Zack grinned sheepishly and said, "Excuse me. I'm convinced."

"How about musterin' us into your outfit?" Ernie asked Del. "Or is that against the rules, too?"

"Not when I need scouts. Anybody know them hills?"

Zack answered. "They're part of Ridge's range. He figures they're in a blind canyon he knows about that's got a spring and grass enough to keep horses several weeks."

"He's head scout," Del said promptly. "The rest of you're his general staff."

"By damn," Ernie said with a chuckle. "Somebody's gonna be sorry they worked so hard to make this look like Injun work."

"Any chance to surprise 'em, Ridge?" Del asked his prospective father-in-law.

"Dead easy; and if we can catch 'em there, they can't get away from us. It's a box canyon."

"Lead on."

They were soon moving, the four civilians riding in the lead with Del. It was something those who had undergone the night's experience had awaited all morning in cold anger. Zack doubted that, if they found their quarry where expected, they would be lucky enough to catch the Sleepers there, too. But a good chance remained of cutting Purdy's gang back to a size where it could be handled.

There was also a chance that the renegades kept their own lookout on one of the Moccasin peaks and were aware of the army detachment's return to the Wagonwheel. If so, they would watch to see where it went from Pistol Peak. So Ridge struck out over Pistol Pass before turning south. In the concealment of buttes and gully washes, the patrol rode swiftly, Ridge's familiarity with his home ground serving well. After a long while of that, Ridge plunged deeper into the hills and in only a few minutes pulled down.

With a forward motion, he said quietly, "The north rim of the canyon's just ahead." He nodded toward a descending defile on the right. "We can follow that down and swing in on the mouth. If we're quiet about it, we might make it before they catch on."

Del nodded and turned to his men. "You heard him; so watch your gear." To the civilians, he added, "If you boys forget we're chasin' Modocs, I could have some tall explainin' to do to the C.O."

Ernie said heartily, "It's your patrol."

They went down through a dark ravine that dropped swiftly and roughly, requiring great care if they were not to betray their presence. At the foot of the passage they came out into one of the grassy bays behind the first foothills. The box canyon was only a short distance to the left. After they reached it, stealth became unimportant: the quarry was either caught inside or had not been there at all.

They rode in boldly through a narrow but widening neck and all at once came into an open space nearly sealed in by rimrock. A fire burned at the base of the right-hand bluff. Zack saw that the rising smoke was carried south, which was why they had not smelled it when up on the opposite rim. There were six men at the fire, all shoved to their feet and staring. There were saddle horses deeper in the enclosure, but none of the smaller Indian ponies. Zack had not expected them to keep the latter on hand after the aborted raid. But these were not all the men who had had a hand in the raid, even with the three Sleepers deducted. This sally couldn't have more than a partial success, whatever Del did about it.

The men at the fire had swept up rifles and seemed balanced between belligerence and diplomacy. They were a hard, dirty-looking lot that undoubtedly had been recruited in one of the tougher mining camps. Del led his detachment calmly toward them. When he stopped, his men pulled up on either side of him. The surprised campers decided on tact.

One, a gaunt man with a hooked nose, said

uncertainly, "What're you army doin' in here?"

"Gettin' ready," Del said, "to ask you people the same question. Don't you know you're in Modoc country?"

"If we didn't when we hit it, we do now." The lanky one let his gaze shift to the others, as if to warn them to let him speak for all. "Nearly run spang into a raid last night. Reckon that's what brought you fellers up this way."

"That's right," Del agreed politely. "How'd you miss it?"

"Well," the hard case said, and shuffled his feet, hard put to answer, "us boys was on our way to Yreka. Got business there. Scared to stick to the emigrant road. Runs too damned near that stronghold everybody's talkin' about. Decided we'd slip around this way at night and miss it. We just come into the pass when we seen buildings burnin' in the basin and knew we'd made a mistake. Found us this place and holed up fast."

"Good thing," Del said. "They killed every white man they run into last night."

The men at the fire couldn't help looking at each other in surprise, for they had run into no white men themselves. The lanky one said uneasily, "They did? That's a shame."

Del nodded, his derisive eyes informing them that he hadn't believed a word he had heard. They shifted themselves worriedly.

"Well, pack up," Del said. "We'll give you an escort as far as the army base. The country from there to Yreka's safe enough."

The lanky man's mouth dropped open. "Hell, that ain't necessary —" he began. The others watched him, annoyed at the way he had let them be trapped. "Don't worry about us, Sergeant. We'll go on tonight on our own."

"You'll come right now. You're in a war theater, and them's orders."

"Now look here!"

Zack didn't hear the order Del must have spoken, but the carbines his men carried snapped up. "Drop your guns," Del told the campers, "and step away from 'em. You're either gonna get safe-conduct or be locked up at headquarters for defyin' martial law."

They were truly hard-bitten men, and if the odds had been less, they might have resisted. For a moment they all stared with bitter, defiant eyes; then one let his rifle fall. The others followed suit, each with his own inner struggle. As they obeyed, they moved away from the fire in obedience to a motioning gun in a trooper's hands. Del spoke to a corporal, who dismounted, gathered the weapons and passed them out for the detachment to carry. At Del's next order the six unhappy campers saddled their horses, including pack animals.

"Now pack the camp," Del said coldly. "Every bit of it." That was as close as he came to telling them he knew there were more of them somewhere around, whom he meant to leave without means of maintaining themselves.

Half an hour later an enlarged party had ridden out into the Wagonwheel and turned north toward Pistol Peak. To the civilians riding ahead with him, Del said quietly, "I'd feel better if it was a clean sweep, but there's no chance of nailin' the rest — who may or may not stick with Purdy, in spite of everything going sour. I'll make sure these boys don't sneak back to join 'em. I'll only give 'em back one gun for self-protection, and the closest place to get more's Yreka. By the time they make it there, they'll be discouraged with the whole business."

"The rest'll have to look to Purdy for equipment and supplies," Ridge reflected. "I sure hope that discourages them, too."

Del left them when they came to Pistol Creek, riding on up the basin with his prisoners, on his way to the new army base at Fairchild's ranch. The other four went back to Zack's place, a little less doubtful of the future than they had been that morning but still somber of countenance. The man whose lust had fastened itself on the Wagonwheel was too bloodily committed to give up, even if the Modocs surrendered or were driven out of the country. The only thing that could end it now was a fight to the death.

While no one thought that the setbacks had diminished Purdy Sleeper's unholy ambitions, the days that followed were as serene as those before so much trouble was visited on the country. Even the Modocs were quiescent, causing various optimists to venture the opinion that somehow they had slipped around the army and shaken the dust of the Tule from their moccasins forever. It was hard even for Zack and his neighbors to maintain the exacting vigilance they had kept up for so long. The thing that held them to their group work by day, and to long watches through the lonely nights, was the thought that their enemy could well be waiting for them to become lulled and careless.

Each morning Zack rode over to Forbidden Canyon, and there had been two weeks more of these fruitless visits when he came out of the creek gorge into the hidden little valley one morning to rein in abruptly. He could hardly believe his eyes as he stared up the creek. Smoke was coming out of the long-unused chimney of the Dunes cabin.

There was only one person who would build a fire there naturally. He almost sent his horse driving forward, when he checked the impulse. Someone might be trying to disarm and lure him into a deathtrap. He rode on, but cautiously, his gun at ready, expecting with every breath to have someone try to shoot him out of the saddle from a hidden point along the trail. Before riding into range of the cabin itself, he sent a shout ringing forward. He had called again before a figure appeared suddenly at the side of the house, looking his way, a slender, wonderful, skirted figure.

Joy broke in his heart, and he went boiling on to her.

"Wendy!"

He had seen her last as a young girl. Now she appeared as a woman, burned brown by the merciless sun of advancing spring, thin from scant rations, worn from a thousand nameless cares. Yet she wore clean clothes, and he knew from the fluffy sheen of her hair that she had just washed it and herself. She stood looking gravely up at him while he swung down, his eyes magnetized.

At last he could say, "You came back."

She looked at the ground, nodding her head, then lifted her eyes. "If you want me, I will be your woman."

"You don't know how I want you," he said softly. "Not as my woman, Wendy — as my wife."

He dropped reins and motioned for her to go into the house. The first thing he noticed when he followed was the combing set he had given her before she ran away from him. She had been using it. He saw that she had fixed herself a meal out of the meager supplies in the cabin.

He said, "When did you come, Wendy?"

"In the dark, last night."

"I've come here every day. Hoping to find you. Hoping I'd get to tell you what I should have before you went away. That I love you."

She looked at him with an expression different from anything he had ever seen in her fine features — different from the timidity she had once shown, from the great courage with which she had looked in such contempt at Monk. It swept

213

away the gaunt, haggard tiredness and restored her youth.

"I love you, too," she whispered. "I will be your wife."

She met him halfway, and there was no reserve in the fierce eagerness of her lips, the close, supple loveliness of her pressing body. She had undergone agony, and out of it had come something magnificently new that was, even so, the girl he had first loved. For long moments she yielded herself to sealing their pledge; then she stepped back, smiling at him.

"I would have been your woman," she said. "I would have worked for you and given you children, and if you no longer wanted me, I would have gone away. For my father was wrong. There are fine men and bad men, and color has no part in it."

Zack nodded. "I never got a chance to tell you, Wendy. But he released you from your promise to go to the Modocs. It was the last thing he ever said."

Her eyes moistened. "I'm glad, but I came back without knowing that. Because my heart told me to."

There had been more to her decision, she went on. After the Modocs had been driven from the stronghold, a great change had come over them. Nearly all of them had believed in the mystic powers of Curly Doctor, but those powers had not saved their fortress in the rocks, had not stopped the soldiers' bullets or replaced either the water in the drying cisterns after the lake was lost or the caches of food they had been forced to abandon in the retreat.

Even Schonchin John had turned against the medicine man, while lesser chiefs like Hooker Jim, Shacknasty Jim, Bogus Charley and Steamboat Frank — all those who had made criminals out of the Modocs to begin with, who had forced Jack into the plot to kill the peace commissioners, whose vote had kept the noncombatants from leaving the lava beds before the second battle — had blamed everyone but themselves for their predicament.

There had been one more upsurge of defiance when the opportunity came to massacre the soldiers at Black Ledge. Victory though that had been, it had failed to reunite the Modocs. The soldier chief Davis, who had replaced the slain Canby, had kept his patrols so continually in the field that it no longer had seemed so simple a thing to hide indefinitely under the noses of the enemy. Hunted relentlessly, abandoned by the Great Spirit, reduced to a state where not a shell could be exploded without serious purpose, growing ever shorter of water and half-starved, the Modocs had decided at last to run for it, hoping they could reach and find refuge in the land of the Shoshones, far to the east. That was as yet a primitive country of vast empty spaces, where nature would feed them and they might be left alone.

The camps had been packed, and the Modocs

had moved in the dark of the night to the southeastern corner of the lava beds. There a temporary camp was to have been set up so the people could rest while waiting until another night to move on into open country. But before the packs had been dropped, advance scouts had returned with a report that was alarming.

Sorass Lake lay on ahead of the main band, and there, the scouts had reported, was camped a large detachment of soldier cavalry, still sleeping except for a few sentries. To the last exhausted waif, the Modocs had known they were in trouble. With soldiers in the immediate vicinity, a crossing of the open country would have been highly hazardous, even at night. Nor could they have waited, hoping that the soldiers would move on the next day, for if they had been discovered where they were, the Modocs would have had to fight off an attack in a bad physical setting. Captain Jack had questioned the scouts, then announced a daring plan.

Again the soldiers had camped on low ground with bluffs all around them, never seeming to have learned the lessons of the broken country. The warriors would attack them from the bluffs at once, hoping to duplicate the success at Black Ledge, which had yielded considerable ammunition. While the attack was in progress, the family band would move on, risking daylight. After crippling, if not destroying, the soldiers, the warriors would join the families and hurry out of the country before the soldiers could reorganize and pursue them. It was desperate but enough like the old days that the people had been heartened, the warriors eager.

At daybreak Jack had opened the attack on the camp at Sorass Lake, pouring in a heavy volley from the bluff above, the taunting whoops of Modocs again ringing over the lava country. Sleeping soldiers had sprung to their feet, some to fling their arms wildly and fall again; the cavalry horses had taken off on the run; and Jack's warriors had accounted for thirteen casualties below them in the opening storm of bullets.

But the soldiers had rallied. There had been many more of them than the scouts had estimated, and they had charged the bluff, forcing the Modocs to pull back and scatter in the rocks. A Modoc had fallen dead in his movement, one of the few who had died in the whole war. But, resettled, the Modocs had stood their ground, hoping to buy time for the families to get away. They had pulled up sagebrush and using it as screens, pushed forward toward the soldiers. It had seemed that they would succeed in their reckless effort when, out of nowhere, a second force of soldiers had appeared. Unknown to the Modocs, this detachment had been camped in the timber on a ridge about a mile from the lake.

There had been altogether too many of them to fight or to elude in flight. Jack had ordered his men to withdraw, and he had turned the main band back into the lavas but in the confusion twenty-four ponies and their packs of food and ammunition had been lost. The Modocs had withdrawn nearly to their old camp at Sandy Butte before the soldiers had given up and withdrawn.

The plight of the Modocs had become worse than desperate. They had known that reinforcements in great numbers would be rushed to the soldiers from the base camp. The renegade chiefs — Hooker, Bogus, Shacknasty Jim and Steamboat Frank — had turned on Jack, berating him for the disaster. But before anything had been settled, the soldiers had attacked again, three hundred and fifty strong, and howitzers had arrived. The Modocs had fought them off until darkness had fallen, and all through the night the big shells had howled and crashed into the rocks. But in the night the Modocs had managed to slip away to the west and emerge from the lavas onto the open plain.

It was over. Wendy, who had attached herself to Hooker's people, had heard them talking in the night. The defecting headmen had agreed to make their way with their followers and families to Fairchild's ranch and there surrender. They would blame Jack and Scarface Charley for everything: the bloody raid down the east side of Tule Lake at the outbreak of the war, the murder of the peace commissioners. They would help track Jack down and testify against him and thus buy their own lives with their lies and treachery.

Captain Jack, left with twenty-five supporters,

had slipped off in the other direction. Surprisingly — and to their credit — Curly Doctor and Schonchin John had still preferred an honorable death as free men and had stayed with Jack. It was then, Wendy said, that she had made up her mind to return to the Wagonwheel. She could not go with Jack, and she would not go with Hooker Jim.

CHAPTER XVIII

Zack listened, with grim eyes, to Wendy's account of the last tragic act of the drama that had played itself to conclusion in the lavas. In it she had learned that good and evil do not reside in separate worlds, that there is only one world, holding every gradation between the extremes. He felt her deep sadness for a cause now lost, for an Indian chief torn down by his inferiors, made a criminal by criminals for their self-preservation and now betrayed by them for the same purpose.

But it was not something he could dwell on for long. Before long, the larger part of the Modoc band would surrender and the news would be spread that Jack and his loyal tatter had fled the country. Once that happened, Purdy Sleeper could no longer try to blame his own evil actions on the Modocs. Before then he would, as he must, strike again.

"You can't stay here, Wendy," Zack said. "I wish you were at Van Bremer's with Dora, but there's no time to take you there. So you'll have to put up with us four men at Pistol Peak. Make a saddle roll of the clothes and things you want to take along."

Her first move was to pick up the combing set he had given her.

She had walked from Sandy Butte in the night, and there was no time to hunt up one of the Indian ponies Martin Dunes had kept around, so they would have to ride double. He went outdoors to see from the sun that he had been inside quite a while. Ernie and the others would be wondering what was keeping him.

She came out, and he lashed the small bundle she had brought behind the saddle seat. After swinging up, he offered a stirrup and hand and brought her up to him. Her slender body, all but carried in his arms, nearly made him forget that the war in the Wagonwheel, instead of being ended, would be brought to its climax by what had happened in the lavas. He turned down the creek toward the gorge.

They were nearly to the dark stricture when sound split through the silence — the sharp, chilling crack of a rifle.

He felt the jerk of Wendy's body, and, in the appalled conviction that she had taken the bullet meant for him, he whipped the horse around, placing his back between her and the rifleman, fully expecting the next shot to put a slug in him. But Wendy twisted, turned her head, and looked up at him with frightened eyes. She was still all right. Spurring, he sent the horse driving back up the creek.

He had barely passed the stricture, making for the upcreek exit, when a shot from that direction jarred the air. He pulled the horse to a ball-footed stop and nearly dropped Wendy bodily in his hurry to get her into cover. He yelled for her to go into the cabin, whose log walls would protect her, meanwhile jerking his rifle out of the boot. His eyes searched the point where the creek broke into the canyon; then they swept the rims on either side. He saw nothing. There were only the two shots. Either one could have killed him, if that had been the only purpose in this.

His flesh chilled when he realized what might account for the restraint. Once he and his partners had picked this place for the ease with which a few men could keep out enemies in superior force. Now someone was using the reverse of that: it was equally possible to hold somebody in Forbidden Canyon a prisoner. In the long moments of his reunion with Wendy, they had been captured by the Sleepers and such hired killers as remained in their service. Purdy had caught on to his daily visits here but had not made use of them until spurred to it by the fact that time was swiftly running out for him.

Zack knew that they meant to keep him here until Ernie, Ridge and Fred rode in to see what had held him up so long. The three were bound to do so, and there was no way to warn them off. Yet maybe there was a way, which was why his captors had been so sparing of their shots. If the three were anywhere near, the sound of shooting would certainly scare them off and enable them to take steps of their own.

The desire to force such shooting was powerful, but Zack reconsidered. He had only the shells in his rifle. He probably could not induce his enemies to return fire, as yet, without exposing himself recklessly that they succumbed to temptations; and if anything happened to him, Wendy would fall into their hands. He thought of Rip and Frank Sleeper, of the lawless hired gun hands. Any of them would treat her as profanely as Monk had intended. He had to think of something better, yet he knew there were few if any possibilities open to him. They had taken him neatly, completely, and they stood to repeat with the three other men who stood between Purdy and full control of the Wagonwheel.

He slapped the horse and drove it over against the east bluff to get it out of the way. He didn't realize that Wendy had come outside again until she spoke at his elbow.

"Who is it? The Sleepers?"

He nodded and turned to see, to his astonishment, that she carried a rifle, an old, eight-shot Spencer. The day he had arrived here to find her father dying, Dunes' rifle had been leaning against the cabin wall. It was a fine gun, tempting to thieves, and he had taken it home, afterward, for safekeeping. He didn't remember seeing the Spencer indoors and said, "You bring that with you last night?"

She shook her head. "Pa knew he'd have to fight 'em off sometime. He had this extra gun and laid in shells for it. We were both gone sometimes, so he fixed a cache in a dry place in the attic."

The Spencer was priceless, even if the shells would not fit Zack's own Springfield. He said, "How much ammunition in that cache?"

"Several boxes."

Zack grinned. "Your father might've saved my partners' lives, and maybe yours and mine, if we're lucky." He told her what he thought their captors were waiting for. Once they had his friends, too, there would be no need for restraint. "It's their last chance to murder us and blame it on the Modocs. Nobody knows where Jack is right now. Purdy'll claim some of that bunch slipped in huntin' for grub and shells, found us here and killed us."

Wendy's eyes closed, but that was her only outward reaction. In recent weeks she had heard the sounds of countless angry guns, had lived with violence and death and things that could be so much worse than death. She said quietly, "I can shoot. Just tell me how to help."

Zack looked around. There was no place in the canyon that could not be reached by a shot from some point on the rims. He told Wendy to go indoors again. He meant to goad whoever was down the creek into trying to silence him. If something happened to him and she remained in the cabin, she could stand them off for a long while with the Spencer. Meanwhile he would have warned his partners away from the deadfall and they would have a chance to rescue her.

What he wanted immediately was noise that would carry to some distance, and his problem was to protect himself from someone who might slip along the rim of one of the side rims. Not far down the creek was what he needed: a pair of boulders he could lie between. They would give him some protection from the sides, and if somebody persisted in trying to root him out, Wendy would catch on to them and drive them back from the cabin window.

It would tempt them to try a shot at him if they saw where he forted up, and he ran forward and dropped into place between the big rocks. He was close enough to the rim of the down-creek gorge to be a nuisance, if not a real danger. He saw nothing, but he lined his sights on a bush up there and fired. The shot rang loudly in the canyon, bouncing off the walls. It drew no audible response or anything otherwise evident.

He waited long moments before he shot again and grinned coldly when, like an echo, his unseen adversaries spanged a bullet off a rock a few feet ahead of him. Again he lay unmoving, meaning only to shoot often enough to give his partners a chance to hear the noise as they approached Forbidden Canyon. He had not yet goaded his enemies enough for them to make a determined effort to silence him, but his third shot brought a bullet that kicked up dust just ahead of his face. He had ammunition enough to keep up the spaced shooting for another half hour; then he would have to retreat to the cabin, take over Wendy's gun, and keep it up as long as Dunes' cache of ammunition held out.

He was down to his last shell when a shot cracked out in a new quarter, loud and near. He realized that it came from the cabin. Wendy had seen something, and she fired twice before silence came again to the canyon. Zack's gaze slid along the west and then the east rim without detecting anything unusual. Then Wendy shot yet again, and it dawned on him that she was firing up the creek, from the far side of the cabin. He hadn't credited the Sleeper bunch with the daring to slip into the canyon behind him, but she had thought of that possibility and guarded against it. She didn't shoot again, so she must have upset that movement.

The sun had come around into his eyes and told him that in another hour it would be high noon. Ordinarily he would have returned to Pistol Peak, or wherever his partners were working, long before now. So it was better than a good guess that, by now, they were looking into his strange absence. There was a fair chance that their failure to blunder into Purdy's trap meant that they were on to it. Zack wished he knew how many men Purdy had with him and what prospect there was of three men managing to defeat his gang.

His last shot brought a retort that Wendy was unable to prevent. The bullet came in from Zack's right, where the rimrock was closer, and when it drove through the calf of his left leg he felt a shock that for a moment rattled his senses.

A second shot came from the west rim, then a third, and he realized that Wendy, required to watch the upstream length of the canyon, had been unable to scan the bluffs directly above him very closely. The additional shots were wide of the mark; then he heard the bark of the old Spencer and there was no more shooting from the west bluff.

He bent his knee and stared at the hole near the top of his riding boot. The whole leg was numb, but the pants leg, underwear and heavy sock inside the boot seemed to be absorbing the blood, since he could neither feel nor see it. He straightened his leg and gave thought to the problem of getting across the open to the cabin, a distance he would have to crawl, with a man on the bluff just above hungering to make the next shot final. Twisting his head, Zack saw that Wendy was standing at the near window. She had broken out the glass for her shot and was motioning for him to come in. She must have had the man on top spotted and though she could keep the fellow from raising up for another shot.

Zack had to expose himself even to turn around and start crawling toward the cabin. The man above must have raised up slightly, for the Spencer cracked wickedly and there was no shot from above. Zack tried to stand up, but for the moment the hit leg was a useless appendage. He began to drag himself over the ground, and Wendy shot twice more at the bluff top before he made it to the door of the cabin. He pulled himself over the threshold and was inside when she interrupted her keen watching and glanced at him.

"Oh — you're hit!"

She hadn't realized that, thinking he had figured it safer to crawl in.

"Nothin' to worry about," he told her. "And you've done a good job. Give me a couple of seconds to get on top of this, and I'll help you."

She turned back but said over her shoulder, "Your friends would have blundered in here by now, wouldn't they?"

"Yeah. I think that part worked."

Zack took out his pocketknife and slit open the top of his boot, leaving the lower part on his foot. The revealed cloth was soggy with blood. When he exposed the wound, he found it in the curve of the calf. The leg had thawed enough to pain him, but he could work the foot and decided that there was no bone damage. He crawled to a chair by the table and pulled himself upright. After putting his knee on the chair seat, he managed to use the chair as a crutch and make his way to the window across from Wendy. At least they had two pairs of eyes, if only one gun for which there was ammunition.

But when Purdy Sleeper gave up hope of trapping the other men, too, he would open up in full fury.

It was around ten-thirty that morning when

Ernie Yost voiced the worry that for some time had been growing in each of the three men branding calves on the south slope of Pistol Peak. They were at a fenced-in spring where, the night before, the cattle using that watering had been penned after coming in to drink. The calves and such slicks as were found in the bunch had all but been worked by midmorning. But instead of proceeding to the end of the job, Ernie suddenly tossed aside the BB branding iron he was using.

"Damn it," he said, his voice vehement with concern. "I never did like that business of Zack changin' his mind about group ridin' and goin' over to Forbidden Canyon by himself."

Ridge nodded glumly. "Well, he was afraid the bunch of us would scare the Dunes girl in case she came back. You thinkin' what I am?"

"That he's been gone too damned long and it's time we found out why."

Fred Trinkler made no comment but was the first to turn toward their horses.

They rode down to the flat and crossed Pistol Creek above the Buckman headquarters. The sun had laid a bright heat on the Wagonwheel and cast a shadowy brilliance on the hills. The three men rode warily. They had not yet heard of the fights at Sorass Lake and Sandy Butte and of the subsequent disintegration of the Modoc resistance. For that reason, they had to allow for Zack's having run into some of the renegade Indians and they slanted sooner than they would have, otherwise, toward the sun-colored rolls of the Coyote Hills. They had reached the cover of the footslope and were riding toward the entrance to Forbidden Canyon when Ernie pulled down his horse.

"Listen!" For a long moment the others joined him in a careful attention. Then Ernie shook his head. "Nothin,' I guess. But I sure thought I heard a rifle shot."

They rode on at a slower gait, silent, each of them straining his ears. There was no more sound of the sort they waited for, yet their worry did not subside. Finally Ridge stopped again and said tensely, "We better be sure what we're gettin' into before we go any nearer."

Then they heard it unmistakable — two shots so close together that the last seemed an echo of the first.

"Which is it?" Trinkler said tightly. "Modocs or Sleepers?"

No further shots followed the two that had been in close succession. Ernie said, "It's Zack for sure, and he's layin' his shots on the heels of somebody else's, or it's the other way round. From what time it is, they've had him there quite a while. And I don't think Modocs would waste a lot of time tryin' to lift just one scalp."

"It's Purdy," Ridge said. "Zack's doin' that spaced-out shootin' tryin' to warn us not to ride into it. They're firin' on the heels of his shots, tryin' to knock him out. Boys, he's usin' up the few shells he's got to save our hides."

"Then they've plugged both ends of the canyon." Trinkler looked around uneasily. "What can we do to help him?"

"Get in," Ridge said, "where we can keep 'em from rushin' Zack after his gun goes dry."

They rode back a hundred yards to where a narrow, rocky canyon cut back into the hills. The footing was steep and broken, and they had to dismount and lead their horses. The defile topped out on a timbered ridge free of underbrush. They remounted and rode swiftly along the ridge until, once more, they heard oddly twinned shots from Forbidden Canyon. Leaving the horses, they moved on afoot and were nearly to the canyon's east rim when a flurry of shots rang out. They went on in on the run and dropped flat at the lip of the rim.

Whispering, Ernie said, "There's Zack. Crawling toward the cabin. He's hit or out of shells. And who's that beyond the broken window, covering him?"

"It's the girl," Ridge, next to him, exclaimed. "She come back finally. And to what a welcome."

"What next for us?"

"Purdy must've seen us coming from Pistol Peak. We'll try not to let him know where we went after we disappeared till they rush the cabin. Which they will now, any minute. They know they ain't gonna get us in there, too."

CHAPTER XIX

It seemed to Zack that he and Wendy had kept up their unblinking watch for half an hour when, for only a second, he saw something move up the creek. The ground in that direction was more broken than downstream, the cliffs verging so that their detritus cluttered the brushy bottom. With his eyes fixed on the spot where he had seen the movement, he spoke quietly.

"Reckon I need the Spencer, Wendy."

At that moment a bullet splintered the window sash while the bright, loud report of a rifle carried to him.

Wendy called, her voice sounding cooler than he felt, "They're moving in on this side, too. I saw one a minute ago, too far off to shoot at."

For an instant Zack closed his eyes. Were he alone, he could be satisfied with exacting the highest price he could for his life. But there was Wendy, and he couldn't let them take her alive, no matter what he had to do to prevent it.

On top of the rest, new guns opened up on the east rim.

He sighed, then creased his brow puzzledly when he realized that the latest volley had not hit the cabin. Still watching up the creek, he heard Wendy shoot; then she sped across to him. He grabbed the rifle and hammered a shot at the spot where he had seen something stir. It brought a flurry in response, and those bullets plowed into the wall around the window. Another volley came from up the creek, and with it an excited yell.

"Hey! Them ain't our men on the east cliff!"

Zack breathed a silent prayer of gratitude, but at that point the men moving up from the gorge began firing. A deep voice up the creek shouted at them, "I tell you, it's a bushwhack! Pull back!"

Somebody showed himself recklessly, up the creek, and Zack shot again. The brush screening the view bent over, and a man stumbled into sight, turned completely about, and fell on his back.

Zack yelled, "It's my partners on the east bluff, Wendy. We've got a fightin' chance."

He shoved the chair aside, tried his hit leg and found that the knee no longer buckled. He hobbled to the other window to discover that the men on that side were ignoring the cabin and shooting at the bluff top. He could see chips of rock fly away up there. His partners would keep this side of the cabin tied up for a while, and he could concentrate on the other.

He went back to the north window, his leg dragging but holding him up. He was in time to spot a man making a forward run toward the cabin. He shot and missed, for the fellow made it to the cover of the rock by the creek, from behind which Monk Sleeper had murdered Martin Dunes. His lips pinched, Zack reflected that it was fitting for the showdown to be here, where Dunes had died under a coward's gun.

The man who had ducked behind the rock was a big fellow wearing a mane of red hair and a bushy beard the same color. So the Sleepers must be down the creek with maybe others, and whoever had been on the west rim a while ago must have joined one group or the other. He wondered how many men had been upstream from the cabin, and a moment's watching showed him nothing more. His breath held, he exposed himself more boldly at the left side of the window, where he was cut off from the man behind the rock. He drew no shot from upstream, not even when he moved into plain sight of anybody up there.

He called Wendy over to him and gave her the Spencer. "Stand on the right side of the window and watch that boulder by the crick. There's a fellow behind it — I think the only one upstream. I'm going to try and tempt him to show himself to you. Or would you rather not have the job?"

"It's as much my job as yours," she returned.

Zack got his empty Springfield and crossed to the door, adjusted to his bad leg so that now he handled it almost unconsciously. The rock was in perfect position for a dead-aim shot at anything around the door, as Monk had proved when he fired the bullet that couldn't miss Wendy's father. Zack moved to the left side of the door opening and then let the rifle barrel tip down and show in the doorway a second before he jerked it back up.

The Spencer roared.

When Zack pulled back and swung toward her, Wendy was looking at him rather than out the window, proof enough that the keyed-up man out there had struck at the bait. Zack hurried to her and put his arm across her shoulder. She was trembling.

"Good girl. Sure of him?"

"I — couldn't have missed."

Zack turned to look out the window and saw that she was right. The redbeard lay on his back out there, with half of his body showing.

"Up to another job?" Zack said gently. She nodded. "Then I want you to slip out of here. I think it's clear up the crick, but I'll make sure."

Spiritedly she said, "I'm not leaving you alone."

"But I want you to make your way up to Ernie and them. Tell 'em one of them can get down here with me. If the other two sneak down to the gorge, we've got Sleeper's bunch hemmed in the way they had us."

Once she understood, Wendy did not object again. Sure that the men on the bluff had those on the bottom tied up for the moment, Zack replenished the empties in the Spencer, then hobbled out of the cabin and up the creek for a distance to be sure that one of the ruffians was not lying doggo. When he was convinced it was safe for her, he sent Wendy on up the creek by herself.

He returned to the cabin, relieved to have her out of a situation that had seemed utterly hopeless. But, although the odds were better, he knew that the fury and violence here were far from spent. The shooting on the south side had settled to a searching, frugal exchange. When he surveyed the scene from the shattered window on that side, he found that Sleeper's men were paying no attention to the cabin at the moment.

The unexpected assault from the bluff had frozen them where they were when it opened. They had crawled into the nearest cover that would protect them from the searching fire from above. Smoke puffs and tendrils gave Zack a count of four men forted up down there and shooting at the rim. If that was all the help Purdy had left, the odds were even for the first time since he had loosed his greed in the Wagonwheel.

Zack decided to hold fire until it became necessary to cut off their escape by way of the upper creek. So he waited there through a period so long that he began to worry about Wendy. But finally the shooting from the bluff broke off. Zack let his shoulders down. She had reached his partners, and they liked his suggestion.

"Hey, Purdy!" a voice on the bottom called. "Looks like they pulled out!"

On the heels of that, a voice — unmistakably Purdy's — rang out. "Red! Red Harris! What's goin' on up your way? Red? Hey — !"

There was a moment's silence, a quality that was magnified after so much echoing gunfire.

Then a man rose cautiously, looking toward the cabin, unsure whether there was anyone left alive there, since no shooting had been coming from it. The man was Frank Sleeper, and Zack held fire until Frank spotted him and lifted his rifle hastily. The Spencer crashed out, and Frank went down in an all-gone fall.

"They killed Frank!" Rip's excited voice yelled. "Let's get outta here! They're tryin' to plug us in!"

There was no telling if Purdy agreed, for all that followed was silence. There was enough cover for them to move down the creek by crawling, but by the time they reached the gorge it would be closed to them. The area around the cabin was more exposed, yet the upper exit from the canyon was much closer. If they could get by the cabin, they probably could move on out of the trap before anyone on the bluff top could get around to contest them. Zack braced himself against their probable decision.

When the long silence ended, it was in a spasm of noisy fury. All of the three men left alive out there concentrated their fire on the cabin window. Zack wheeled back so violently that his bad leg buckled and he went down hard.

He must have flung up an arm that showed, for Purdy yelled, "By God, we got him! Come on!"

Zack had trouble getting up but made it and, grabbing the rifle he had dropped, lurched drunkenly to the door. And there, hurrying up the creek on that side, was Purdy. They spotted each other in the same instant. Purdy let out a blurting "Hey — !" and then jerked up his rifle in the same breath in which Zack shouldered the Spencer.

The two explosions seemed one. Metal tore into a log at Zack's ear, while Purdy's hate-twisted face went slack and flat. Before Zack could shoot again, he saw there was no need. Purdy's arms relaxed, the rifle dropped, and then Purdy fell across it. When the echoes of the shots died out, Zack heard bodies crashing through the brush. The other two had gone up the far side of the cabin and got by him. Zack went hobbling after them, realizing in only a moment that pursuit, in his condition, was useless. He halted and went back to Purdy, who was shot through the center of his chest and dead.

Then two shots rang out up the creek, and Zack straightened, waiting for more. There were no more. He knew that somebody from the rim had got around in time to block the escape. A few minutes later Ernie came down the creek with his gun barrel jammed into the back of a man Zack had never seen.

"Got Rip," Ernie said tersely. "This'un had had enough and gave up. He'll help set the record straight on what's been goin' on in the Wagonwheel."

A few minutes later Ridge and Trinkler came up the creek, Wendy with them. They found five dead men in the canyon, and three of them were the last of the Sleeper clan.

Ridge voiced what all of them felt. "All Captain Jack ever asked for was the freedom these lobos had. Till the white people made him a lobo, too, I'd sooner've had Jack for a neighbor. It makes a man wonder where they get the idea it's the white folks who deserve this country."

Del took a turn around the room, halting finally to glare at his brother. "Don't know how you manage to stay so cool. I'm scareder than I ever was in them lava beds." He looked strange in a suit of civilian clothes after having clad his big frame so many years in the blue of the army, which he had put behind him now for good.

Zack stood at the window, also in his best attire, looking off across Pistol Creek toward the far Coyote Hills. He was thinking that the range over there, which Martin Dunes had claimed, now belonged to Wendy. She in turn had put it at his and Del's disposal. There would be room for a cattle ranch more than capable of supporting two families, and he had just been hoping that they would be large families.

"If you'd rather not get married, Del," he said, "I can tell Dora, when I ride over, that it'll have to be a single wedding because you boogered out."

"I'm boogered," Del said, grinning. "But not out."

Zack looked back at the far hills, happier than he could remember ever being, yet feeling a trace of sadness. Del had been in on the last act before the curtain rang down for Captain Jack and had told him about it. The Modocs who had brought Jack to ruin, and then turned traitors, had led the army to his hide-out on the headwaters of Willow Creek, beyond Goose Lake. There, cornered, his few remaining followers exhausted and starving, Jack had surrendered. His whole band had been taken to the peninsula at Tule Lake to be hung, but last-minute orders had come from Washington for them to be moved to Fort Klamath and given a trial. Only those who had taken part in the murder of the peace commissioners were to stand trial, and the traitors had saddled that on Jack and those who had stayed with him. There was no doubt that they would be hung.

That was a sadness, Zack thought, that would have its effect on Wendy, too, on their wedding day. She was over at Dora's, where she had lived since their bloody experience in Forbidden Canyon. The two girls were now like sisters and had worked night and day to make Wendy a wedding dress to match Dora's. Ridge had sent the word far and wide and ranchers would be gathering at his place already from every direction. The preacher had ridden out from Yreka the day before.

Del was looking at his watch, as he had done a dozen times in the last hour. This time he said with satisfaction, "Time to go, if we're gonna get there when they said."

Zack walked over to get his hat, still limping slightly on his newly healed leg. Then they left to claim their brides.